THICKER THAN WATER

By the same author

Robert Estienne, Royal Printer. Cambridge University Press, 1954.
Revised edition, Sutton Courtenay Press, 1986.

Ronsard and the Age of Gold. Cambridge University Press, 1968.

Before Copyright: The French Book-privilege System 1498–1526. Cambridge University Press, 1990.

THICKER THAN WATER

Elizabeth Armstrong

The Book Guild Ltd
Sussex, England

This book is a work of fiction. The characters and situations in this story are imaginary. No resemblance is intended between these characters and any real persons, either living or dead.

The Book Guild Ltd
25 High Street,
Lewes, Sussex

First published 1998
© Elizabeth Armstrong, 1998

Set in Baskerville by
Rowland Phototypesetting Ltd,
Bury St Edmunds, Suffolk

Printed in Great Britain by
Antony Rowe Ltd, Chippenham, Wiltshire

A catalogue record for this book is
available from the British Library

ISBN 1 85776 224 X

1

The Provost of St Matthew's College, a former senior civil servant, Sir James Egerton, generally known even in his own family as 'J.E.', who had returned some five years previously to head his old college, had made it known that he would not be dining with the fellows that evening. He had the reading of some prize essays, for which he was an examiner, to finish, and wanted some uninterrupted time to himself.

The member of the staff who acted as his butler was laying the table in the Small Dining Room.

All at once the bell rang at the front door of the Lodgings on the street. The butler went to answer it. A dark young man he did not know asked to see the Provost. He was good-looking, well set up, well-dressed and well-spoken, and carried an impressive briefcase. But there was a somewhat wild-eyed look about him.

Warily, the butler asked, 'What name, sir?'

'John Egerton. His son,' answered the visitor, impatiently.

As he took his hat off to come in, the butler observed a strong resemblance to the portrait which hung over the fireplace in the Provost's study and which he knew to be the late Lady Egerton.

He said, 'I beg your pardon, sir. I know your brothers, of course. I don't think we have met before. I will tell the Provost at once.'

But already the door of the study had opened and the Provost's tall silhouette had appeared in the lighted doorway.

1

He called out, 'John? What a pleasant surprise. Greenfield, we shall be two for dinner.'

In the study, John confronted his father. Unlike his elder brothers, whom he detested, he had never got on with him. Only his mother had prevented an open rebellion and she had been killed in a traffic accident when he was in his last year at the university. Once he had set up on his own in the City, he broke with him entirely, hung up on his phone calls, ignored his letters and declined to attend any family functions.

He said, almost truculently, 'I suppose you think I wouldn't be here unless I wanted something. If so you suppose right. I happen to be in imminent danger of going broke, or worse.'

'What's the trouble?' asked the Provost.

'The trouble is a building project in France which has taken longer to complete than I expected. Henri de La Bastide put me on to it. You will remember him, probably. He was with us in the holidays to learn English. He's now the leading light in the family firm of notaries. Has a charming wife. I stay with them often. He knew of a man in Berry whose *château* had been burnt down and who had used the insurance money to clear that site and to begin building a modern house there, with one or two houses further away in the park. He had a first-rate Paris architect and the plans are brilliant. But he ran into financial difficulties and was eventually forced to put the whole property on the market. I went over it with Henri. It was simply lovely. I was pretty flush with funds then, having just sold a couple of houses very well. I decided to buy it and to take over the plans. It seemed a bargain. – Oh, this must sound crazy to you. Of course you don't know the background.'

John began to walk up and down the room, talking feverishly.

'I have been in house property as a sideline, on my own, for several years. It began as a lark. Then I got hooked on it. I got the hang of what people wanted and what they would pay for. I found good houses in need of modernizing, or even rebuilding, in unfashionable areas but within easy reach of London. They could be bought for a song. I got to know the ways of builders and plasterers and carpenters and electricians and plumbers and heating engineers. I recruited self-employed men who were glad to have a job and were cooperative about working hours as long as they were well-paid. I learnt to deal with planning committees and such like. It only needed some entrepreneurial know-how – and good taste. It was great fun. And it was more and more successful. I thought the Berry project would require much the same skills, that I would only have to get up some technical terms in French. But in France I had to use a small local firm of contractors who were already on the job and pay them at intervals as we went along. They had made a good impression on me. And they did have good workmen and were basically honest. But they were unbelievably slow. My success until then had been due, much more than I realized, to being *there*. I used to be on the site first thing in the morning and go over the day's programme with them, every day, and chivvy them at other times if necessary. I could only get over to Berry for a day or two every other week, at best, without neglecting my work in the office. The blighters fell more and more behind schedule. I counted on the main house, the replacement *château*, being finished and sold by now. Instead I'm still having to pour money into it and have nothing yet to show for it. The latest news is that they don't expect to have the roof on until January, and then only 'weather permitting'. And I had begun work on the foundations for the second house and the approach road to it: at the time, it seemed more economical. Of course, when the new *château* is something like finished, I ought to be able to sell it and it should fetch at least a million. But I can't expect anything back until then and I have simply run out of cash.'

'You couldn't get a bridging loan?' asked the Provost.

'That's probably what I ought to have done. But I was relying on some investments to cover all eventualities. When I *did* need the money, I had to sell at a particularly bad time.

3

They fetched far less than I had counted on. By then, I couldn't even have serviced a loan.'

John paused.

'And so I borrowed, as a last resort, from the source nearest at hand. It would be only for a few months. It seemed quite safe. And then by sheer bad luck several clients gave notice that they would want soon to realize a lot of their assets. The most pressing of them, a Major Thomas, has taken it into his head to buy a house to retire to and needs £275,000. He is already impatient and now he has threatened me with a solicitor's letter unless he has satisfaction by the end of next week. And then the fat will be in the fire.'

The Provost's eyebrows went up.

'Speculating with clients' money, John? Unwise, surely, as well as wrong. What will you do? Can you sell the French property?'

'Even if I could find a buyer at such short notice, I would only get a fraction of its value, nothing remotely like £275,000. The main house is all in scaffolding and the second one looks like a bombed site, with JCBs groaning round it in the mud.'

'Isn't there any agricultural land with it?'

'No. The family sold that. There is only the park.'

'You have a flat in London?'

'Yes. I rent a furnished flat. The lease come up for renewal next month.'

'And you've sold all your investments?'

'Yes.'

'Bank account?'

'Current balance is a few hundred. Frankly, I'm desperate. J.E., can you . . . will you, help me?'

'I don't rule it out,' answered the Provost. 'But I must have facts and figures. We must talk business. Not now. This will need a lot of thought. Have dinner and spend the night here. In the morning we will see what can be done.'

'I'm not hungry,' said John, fretfully. 'And how could I spend the night, even if I wanted to? You weren't expecting me and I haven't brought anything with me.'

4

'Wise heads of houses always have a bed made up and aired: one never knows who may arrive. I'm sure we can produce a toothbrush and a shaver. And you can borrow a pair of my pyjamas: they won't be much too big for you. Now, come and have a wash.'

John had spent the previous night and most of the morning pacing the streets of London sick with ever-intensifying despair. Having decided, at the last extremity, to try his father, he had pulled himself together to the extent of getting a shave and had swallowed a large cup of black coffee before catching the train.

Now, as he began mechanically to eat and drink what was set before him, his natural combativeness tried to reassert itself. He started to make conversation, almost insolently.

'How do you like being Provost? Not too arduous, I suppose?'

'It is quite arduous, especially in term,' answered his father. 'But yes . . . I do like it.'

'Has the college changed a lot since your day?'

'Not more than I expected. I have always kept in fairly close touch with it, as an ordinary old member.'

'It's a mixed college now, I take it?'

'Has been for several years.'

'How do you find that?'

'I find it very civilized. Let me give you some more claret, John.'

'Yes, please. It is excellent.'

When they had finished coffee, the Provost said, 'You're interested in houses. Would you like to see something of this one before you go to bed?'

John assented.

The dining room, lined with portraits of college worthies, and encumbered with a massive table and numerous heavy chairs, was monumental rather than elegant. The parlour, on the other hand, showed the style of the house to advantage. A magnificent oriental carpet stretched almost the whole length of the room and it was furnished with good

5

antique pieces and pleasing pictures. A semi-professional interest stirred within John.

'Nice proportions. About 1820?'

'That's right. Provost White, who built it, moved into it in 1823.'

John stopped, at random, by a marble-topped table, with a picture hanging above it which he recognized.

'Some of these things come from the drawing room at home?'

'Nearly all. This room was unfurnished except for some tattered old curtains. It all had to be done up. And to me it was one of the attractions that there was space in the house for our own things.'

They returned to the entrance hall.

'I have breakfast at 8.15 and see my secretary at 9.00,' said the Provost. 'You will be brought breakfast upstairs and you can bath and dress at your leisure. Then we will discuss matters.'

Having dispatched his son, the Provost went back to his study. But he did not immediately return to his prize essays. He walked slowly over to the fireplace and looked for a moment at the portrait of his wife. Then he sat down at his desk, took out a sheet of paper and began to write.

The next morning, John opened his briefcase and laid bare the full extent of his predicament.

The Provost asked, 'You have a partner?'

'Of course. Betsy Howard. She is the senior partner, in fact. She is the niece of old man Andrews, who was head of the firm when I came and taught me the job. She is first-rate.'

'Hasn't she smelt a rat?'

'I've no reason to think so.'

'She must be very trusting.'

'I hope not. But she trusts *me*.'

'And can we trust *her*? It is only a matter of days – perhaps hours – before she finds out. If you and I reach an agreement, shan't we have to put our cards on the table with her?'

'She is a pillar of rectitude. I am sure she wouldn't agree to anything dubious.'

'She won't have to, if we can meet all your obligations to your clients, will she? And it is probably in her interests that the firm should stay afloat?'

'Very much so. She is not badly off, but she has three school-age children and her husband died last year.'

'Poor woman. She is in for a shock. But I think we can assume she will cooperate. Let us talk business.'

The Provost looked shrewdly at his son.

'You are a clever man, John, though in this matter you have not been quite clever enough. I think you are also possibly a dangerous man. If you have treated your clients in this way – and how do I know that this is the first time? – what reason have I to rely on you to treat me any better? If I have to put down £275,000 immediately, and more soon, and that will be a large proportion of my fortune by the look of it, to help you, I shall have to protect myself by making very stringent terms.'

'Fair enough. What are your terms, J.E.? I do intend to repay you as soon as I can, but I realize that you have no reason to believe me.'

'I shall not refuse repayment, if you are ever in a position to offer it,' said the Provost. 'But I am a realist. Even if your French project is sound – and I have no means of judging that at present, though the plans you have shown me look all right – it may be a long time before you can repay such a debt. I might be dead by then. No, I am going to require you to do certain things which I want, for the next year.' He picked up the sheet of paper on which he had been making notes the previous evening. 'In the first place, you will take unpaid leave of absence from the business for a year on grounds of health – we will say that you have been overworking and that your doctor wants you to have several months' rest. We will ask Mrs Howard to run the office with any additional help she may need.'

John frowned, but he nodded.

7

'Yes. I can understand that you want to keep me out of business.'

'And you will give up your flat in London, at once.'

Again he tried to be reasonable.

'Of course, I see that you wouldn't want to pay for an expensive flat in Town for me. But where am I to live?'

'With me. Here.'

'You're joking. That's preposterous.'

'Not at all. You will be treated with the same consideration as any other guest staying in my house. No one except ourselves will know the real reason why you have come. Everyone will think it quite natural that you should stay here when you have been ordered a rest.'

'But how could I possibly adapt?'

'Very simple. You will follow the routine I approve. You will behave with civility to everyone and, in public, to me. And "everyone" includes your brothers and their families, who are very much part of my life.'

'You are asking me to become a monster of duplicity.'

'I am asking you to play a part. You may find it a demanding part, at least at first, and you will be on stage for a lot of the time. But don't tell me you can't act. I've seen you too often in productions at school and at the university.'

'I couldn't act the part of "loving brother" to Fred and Richard, whatever you say.'

'I said, "with civility", not necessarily with affection. That might even be overplaying the part.'

John's thoughts reverted to the subject of money.

'I may keep my bank account, such as it is, I suppose?'

'Yes. But you will show me your bank statements and any cheques that you write. And all correspondence.'

'Business correspondence, of course.'

'*All* correspondence.'

'You don't mean that you expect to see my private letters?'

'Certainly I do. How otherwise can I be sure that I know what you are up to?'

John exploded.

'You wouldn't try to impose such a condition even on a teenage daughter.'

'I probably wouldn't have to. To judge by what I have seen of other people's daughters, she might get herself into a mess, but I doubt whether it would have been such an expensive mess. Now, listen. If, having accepted my help on these conditions, you fail to keep your side of the bargain, I shall stop keeping mine. I will make no further payments for you and I shall ask you to leave here within a week. If you keep it, you will walk out of the house in twelve months' time a free man, whether you have repaid me or not, and you need never see me again if you don't want to.'

John drew a deep breath.

'You mean that? It is a promise, J.E.?'

'It is a promise, yes. And if you find at any time that you can repay me, naturally the whole agreement will lapse. I have put all this down in black and white. If you accept my terms, please sign and date the paper. It has no legal force. But it will forestall any argument about the agreement.'

John took the sheet of paper from him and read what was written on it. As he saw the conditions in writing, and fully realized the indignities to which he might be exposing himself, he jumped to his feet.

'This is monstrous. Vindictive. Sadistic. You just want to have your revenge for what you no doubt regard as my bad behaviour to you.'

'My motives are mixed,' answered the Provost. 'It so happens that revenge, as you call it, is not one of them. There is nothing to avenge. You had a perfect right to go your own way. That your way ended up on the edge of a precipice is unfortunate for us both.'

John argued. Angry and distraught, he even at one point swore at his father. The Provost refused to be provoked. But he continued to insist on his own terms.

Finally, at bay, John declared, 'I would rather go to prison than put up with such a life.'

'That seems to be the alternative,' said the Provost, mildly. 'It is for you to choose. Take your time.'

9

There was a long pause. John knew that he was beaten, at least for the moment. He suspected that his father, whatever he said, might be satisfied with having inflicted such a humiliation on him. He began to think, too, that the more objectionable of his conditions might well prove impossible to enforce.

With the utmost reluctance, he put his signature and the date at the bottom of the paper. The Provost took it, and put it away in his desk.

Then he said, 'Now, hadn't you better telephone Major Thomas and make your peace with him, if you can?'

'I may tell him that he will have his £275,000 by the end of next week?'

'Certainly. Go ahead. Dial 9 for an outside line.'

John picked up the telephone and dialled. He already felt better. Business was the breath of life to him, and a business dealing, even when he expected a battering from a justifiably incensed client, found him playing the smooth operator with coolness, almost with relish. He made no excuses.

'All my apologies – most vexatious for you – inexcusable inefficiency on my part – everything is in order now – yes, by the end of next week without fail – no problem.'

As he put the telephone down, the Provost said, 'Good. Now we must put our minds to ways and means. I'll ring up my broker . . . but not immediately. I want to draw up a plan first. Then if he has anything better to suggest, well and good. I'll get out my most recent portfolio and valuation. You must help me, John. After all, aren't you an expert? Fetch this morning's paper so that we can see the prices. You keep the score on a bit of paper. Here. Fixed interest? Not a good moment to sell, I think? We may have to come back to them. Let's look at the equities . . .'

For three quarters of an hour father and son, their differences temporarily forgotten, were wholly absorbed in the technical problem of selling to the best advantage to produce the desired sum. After careful discussion, several of the Provost's largest holdings were selected. He pondered a moment.

10

'Martin is a personal friend. I had better have an explanation handy for wanting to raise such a large sum so quickly. I shall tell him that I am backing an enterprise of yours in France. It's not far from the truth. And will explain too why I want it paid to you. Should it be to your personal account, or to the firm's?'

That point settled, the Provost telephoned.

'James Egerton here. Oh, fine, thanks. How's the market this morning? I want to do some selling. My son John is into an important property development in France and I have agreed to help him finance it . . . Oh, he has been in this line of business quite a long time, very successfully.'

John gave a wry smile.

His instructions to the broker duly given, the Provost said, 'And now for your unfortunate partner.'

'You're surely not going to tell her everything on the phone?' expostulated John.

'Of course not. And anyway you must speak to her yourself. We will arrange to see her in your office tomorrow.'

'Tomorrow?'

'Yes. I have checked that I have nothing on tomorrow that cannot be postponed. We will see her together and then go to your flat and pack your things. Get on to her.'

Even the Provost, some distance away, heard the cry of relief from Mrs Howard.

'Oh, John, where *have* you been? Where are you? I have been so worried. I had several calls from your client, Major Thomas, who seemed very vexed that he hadn't had a reply to the letter which he had sent you about realizing some of his investments. I couldn't find his letter, and could only say that I was trying to contact you but I feared you must be ill or had an accident.'

'I am so sorry you have been anxious, Betsy,' said John, in his most reassuring tone. 'I had to go unexpectedly to see my father. I have Major Thomas's letter with me, and I have just telephoned him. I shall be in the office by – what time, J.E.? – by 11 o'clock. You will be free? Good. Goodbye for now.'

*   *   *

11

At 11 o'clock the next day they walked into the office in London. Mrs Howard was pleased but surprised to meet John's father. John grasped the nettle at once.

'About that letter from Major Thomas.'

'Yes, indeed,' said Mrs Howard, reproachfully. 'I can't understand why you hadn't sent him a reply. The money's there.'

'Only on paper, I'm afraid. I must come clean, Betsy: I have been having a flutter with it. A property development which I have in France is costing more than I expected and won't start giving returns for a few months. So to bridge the gap . . .'

Mrs Howard stared at him. She went pale under her make-up.

She said faintly. 'Oh, *no*. Not that. You, of all people, John!'

'But no one is going to suffer,' said John. 'My father has generously undertaken to bail me out.'

The Provost intervened. John had been overworking. He needed a complete rest. The plan was, that he should take unpaid leave for at least several months and convalesce with his father. She was going to be asked to run the business during that time, with whatever extra help she might need in the office.

Mrs Howard thought.

'As long as I am not being required to do anything illegal, Sir James . . .'

'Something illegal *has* taken place, certainly. But there is no reason why anyone except the three of us should ever know that. John will have, probably by tomorrow, the means to send the money on the firm's behalf to Major Thomas. And any other obligations to his clients will be fully covered.'

After some further discussion, Mrs Howard fully regained control of the situation.

'You mentioned extra help. Yes, I shall need that, if I am to be responsible for John's work as well as mine. We have a very good secretary and an excellent shorthand typist. But

12

we shall want someone who knows about investments.'

'What shall we do? Advertise?'

'We want someone quickly. I should like to offer the job, for a year, to a girl I know well personally who has suitable qualifications. She was in the investment department of a bank, but was recently made redundant. I have acted as a reference for her for two or three posts that she has tried for – of course the competition is intense. I have her CV which I can show you. I am sure she would jump at the chance of even a temporary appointment like this.'

'Then I don't think we need look any further, do you, John? Shall we leave Mrs Howard to negotiate with her about salary and so on? Now we have only to give you John's address and telephone number with me . . .'

At John's flat, having arranged for the termination of the lease, and the forwarding of his possessions and his post, they set about packing those of his things which would go into his suitcases. Halfway through, the key turned in the lock and a young woman came in, smartly dressed and heavily made up.

'Oh, there you are, darling. Wherever *have* you been? When I couldn't find you, I went to stay with a friend and took my belongings there, because I didn't know what had happened to you.' Then she stopped, seeing that they were not alone.

'Won't you introduce us, John?' said the Provost.

John bit his lip.

'Serena, this is my father, Sir James Egerton. J.E., this is Miss Serena Smith.'

The girl, finding herself with a handsome and obviously successful middle-aged man, smiled benignly, and shook hands, saying, 'Pleased to meet you, Sir James. Now I know where John gets his good looks from.'

'You are mistaken, Miss Smith. They happen to come from his mother. But now, we have some serious news for you. John has been overworking. His doctors want him to have a complete rest. For several months. He is going to close the flat, and come and live with me, for the time being. I will explain . . .'

He was already piloting her firmly to the door and in a few moments it shut behind them. John thought of going after them, but the passage was a risky place to make a scene and he told himself that he would easily find the means to contact Serena later. After several minutes, the Provost returned alone.

'A very reasonable young lady,' he pronounced. 'I asked her whether it would be a hardship to her to have to stop seeing you at such short notice and to make other plans. She said, yes, it would, rather. We talked a little. I got her to name a specific sum. I had brought a lot of money with me in cash today, because I didn't know what might be needed. So I gave her what she asked. She sat down on a chair by the lift and counted the banknotes over most carefully. Then she gave me her latchkey to the flat and we parted *à l'amiable.*'

'The devil you did. You have no right to interfere in this high-handed way, J.E. Serena is part of my private life.'

'Not any more. Now, finish packing that case and come along, or we shall miss the train.'

On the way back, the Provost said, looking up from the evening paper, 'By the way, I am dining in Hall this evening. You will come as my guest.'

'How awful,' commented John. 'I suppose I shall have to meet some of your ghastly colleagues.'

'I don't think anyone too ghastly has signed in tonight. There is Clive Fletcher, the Vice-Provost. He's a historian, originally from University College, London. Can seem a bit brusque but not at all a bad sort. Miranda Elton, one of the English tutors. She knows a lot about the theatre. In fact, has written at least one play herself which had a run in the West End. She is conceited. But quite amusing. The only other one, I think, is Jonathan Sopes. He's a Research Fellow in Economics. Post-Doctoral. Knowledgeable, especially

14

about the Third World. Oh, and I think Robert Austin, the college doctor.'

'And I sit next to you?'

'That's right. I don't know who will be on the other side of you. That depends on who comes there. But I will be able to introduce you to them first, as we meet beforehand. I have already told Clive that you will be staying with me. I haven't had a chance to tell anyone else.'

It was Miranda Elton who came to sit next to him. Not unpleasing, John thought. A few years older than himself. He was still slightly dazed, but revived a little, aided by intelligent feminine company and a good dinner. He began to sound her tentatively about the present state of theatrical life in the university. It soon transpired that she remembered well a production in which he had taken part, not that she claimed to remember him, in what had been only a minor role. But they had a lively conversation about the producer.

After dinner, Dr Fletcher, who had been sitting on the Provost's left, came over to talk to him.

'I'm sorry to hear that you have been overworking and have to take a rest, John – may I call you 'John'? I suppose life in the City can be pretty stressful?'

'I enjoy it. But I suppose I have been enjoying it too much. I shall miss London, though.'

'There's no place like it, is there?'

Afterwards he had some conversation with Jonathan Sopes, who turned out be a genial Jamaican, about his own age.

The next morning, at breakfast, the Provost got out his diary, and said, 'Tonight I shall have to dine in Hall, as I have promised to be there to meet someone else's guest. I'm afraid you will have to have dinner on your own here.'

'I shall go out to a restaurant.'

'No.'

'Why not?'

'Frankly, because I don't yet know how far I can trust you, John. We shall have to get to know each other better before

15

you can go out for the evening except with me or with friends or colleagues of mine. Let's face it: we are virtually strangers.'

'But this is appalling. I am to be a prisoner in your house?'

'Not as bad as that. I don't mind if you want to go out during the day to go to the library, or have your hair cut, or take exercise. Only you will tell me at breakfast where you propose to go and when you will be back. If anything unexpected crops up after that, you will leave me a note.'

'Exercise . . .' John grasped at the word. 'I am used to going for a swim before breakfast. I suppose you will find some reason to veto that.'

'Not at all. I am glad you are keeping up your swimming. We must find out when the baths open.'

'And what am I to do with myself?'

'Keep up with your subject. After all, we hope you will be going back to normal business life in a year's time. And my investments will be in intensive care. Your care. All transactions of course will be done through my broker. But we must make every penny we can.'

This was language which John understood.

'Where am I going to do this, though? You'll need the study yourself, I suppose? I've only got a miserable little bedroom.'

'We'll arrange an office-cum-bedsitting room for you. This is an old-fashioned house, but a large one. There is a big room on the top floor which I have been lending to the college. The last occupant was an earnest graduate who sat up there all day with his word processor. He's got his Ph.D. and gone home. Mrs Mace, the senior daily help, with whom I have had a word, tells me that the eldest daughter of the late Provost had it as her bed-sitting room and that it has good built-in cupboards. There is a bathroom and a pantry across the passage. Read the newspaper and when I have seen my secretary we'll go and look at it.'

In due course John was introduced to the secretary. Then they climbed the stairs to the second floor and met Mrs Mace.

16

The room was shabby. It contained a minimum of student furnishing: a divan bed covered with a dustsheet, a battered table and chairs, an old desk and a threadbare carpet. Used to sizing up superficially poor accommodation, John observed that it was spacious and well-proportioned, with a large window looking over to the college garden. He said he thought it had possibilities.

'That is has, sir,' said Mrs Mace, warmly. 'It just needs a good turn-out and polish-up and for them things of the Bursar's to be took away. It looked real nice when Miss Nancy had it. The bed is sound, sir: *that* belongs to the Lodgin's that does.'

'We'll go out and buy a presentable desk and chairs,' said the Provost. 'The Bursar will be glad to make use of the old ones. The rest of my son's belongings should be delivered early tomorrow. Could you and Mrs Roberts get the room ready for him to move into tomorrow, do you think?'

'Sir,' said Mrs Mace, sternly, 'there's the parlour to be done in the mornin'. The floor and the furniture there won't polish theirselves. I ain't got two pairs of hands, nor Mrs Roberts hasn't.'

The Provost appeared to cogitate.

'Perhaps,' he said, diplomatically, 'the parlour could wait until next week. It looks fine. And then, I shall not be using it until the week after next . . .'

As they came downstairs, the secretary, who had been waiting for them, said, 'I am so sorry, Sir James. There is one thing I forgot. That memorial service for Judge Harris on Saturday week. The arrangements for it were all made last term. But you are giving a lunch party before it. Ten people. Would you mind making the seating plan now? I have the place cards here. Then I could get ahead with making copies of the plan.'

'Certainly,' said the Provost, sitting down at his table. 'The Judge's widow, Lady Harris, on my right. Then there is her sister, and her son and daughter-in-law, and two teenage granddaughters, plus the chaplain and the two Law fellows, Dr John Robins and Miss Goodwin.'

John watched curiously as his father shuffled the cards into two neat rows, alternating ladies and gentlemen. He tried several different arrangements.

'All right, now, except whatever do I am left with the two girls stranded looking across the table at each other at the far end. We can't have that. It would be very dull for them.'

'Shall we invite another of the fellows to take the end of table?' suggested the secretary. 'The Vice-Provost, for instance? He'll be coming in any case to the memorial service, won't he?'

'Poor old Clive. Come to my rescue, John. I am afraid it will be an exceedingly dull party, but, if you are free, would you mind sitting at the end of the table?'

'More entertaining for the granddaughters,' volunteered the secretary.

'If you want me to,' said John, surprised. He thought it would be probably no duller than lunching on his own, which he assumed would be his fate otherwise, and most likely a better lunch.

'Good. That's settled,' said the Provost. 'Lend John your file on Judge Harris, please, Mrs Macrae. You had better do a little homework on this, John. Now, let's go out and interview some furniture for you.'

They chose an office desk and chair, and two small armchairs, and were promised delivery early the next morning.

'You will need a decent rug, too,' remarked the Provost, as they walked back. 'I have a Hamadan rug in the dining room which might do. Or there is a larger one among those in the parlour . . .'

That evening, Greenfield brought John his dinner over from the college kitchen. It was a smarter dinner than he would have at most restaurants in the town, and nicely served. The butler was solicitous and, John thought, a little curious.

'I'm sorry to hear you've been overworking, sir,' he said, as he put the dishes on the sideboard. 'You take after the Provost, sir, if I may say so. He always works ever so hard. It will be nice for him to have you with him though, sir.'

'What makes you think that, Mr Greenfield?' asked John.

'Why, sir, it's a big house for a gentleman on his own. Of course he has a lot of visitors. But there's nothing like one's own family, is there, sir?' And he added, saving John the trouble of a reply, 'Please be so good as to turn the hotplate off when you have finished, sir. I shall come over and clear later.'

After dinner, John wandered moodily into his father's study. On the desk he noticed a framed photograph. It was an enlarged snapshot of the three boys – Fred, Richard and himself – sitting side by side on the sea wall on their last summer holidays together. He scowled at it and went to look at the books on the shelves. There was a fine collection of recent political and diplomatic history, autobiographies of statesmen and other public figures. Some of the latter were presentation copies. One, from an eminent politician, bore the jocular inscription, 'For J.E., with friendly memories of our many disagreements'. John was surprised. He had never taken the slightest interest in his father's career. It had seemed dull, remote and official. He turned to the adjoining shelf which held mainly Continental works of the same kind. At least one of these too was inscribed by the author, a work by André Maurois, who had dined with them in London. Further on, he found the first edition of the memoirs of General de Gaulle. He took it down and began to read it.

About nine o'clock he heard the front door on the college side open and the Provost came in.

'I hope you've had a proper dinner, John. Ah, you're looking at De Gaulle. He wrote well, didn't he? Fine classical French, wouldn't you say?'

'Yes, indeed. Did you ever meet him, J.E.?'

'A couple of times.'

'What was he like?'

'I found him insufferable. But he was a remarkable man.' The Provost switched to present-day French politics. 'The Bastides used to be Gaullist – RPR – as far as I remember. What does Henri think now?'

When he went to bed over an hour later, John realized, suddenly, with something like resentment, that he had been having a normal conversation with his father, of the kind which he might have had with any older man who was intelligent and well-informed about France. He said to himself that he had been caught off his guard.

The following morning they had another session to discuss finance.

'I want to complete covering all your possible obligations to the firm,' said the Provost. 'After that, naturally, we shall continue to have the expenses for your French project. It would be useful for you now to have a look at my income and expenditure.'

John immediately remarked on the Provost's stipend. He was shocked.

'But it's derisory. Hardly more than a backbench MP?'

His father was amused.

'Academic salaries are rarely princely, John. I have, as you see, a few "perks" as well: the use of the house, a tax-free entertainment allowance.'

'Call that an entertainment allowance? It can't endow you with more than two or three lunch-parties a term, and some sherry and peanuts at other times. Can't you get more out of them than that?'

'No. It's a poor college. I knew what I was doing when I took on the job. I realized that I should have to subsidize it to some extent myself, especially the entertaining, if things were to be done as I should like.'

'You must have been getting twice as much as this in the civil service,' John persisted.

'Rather more than that. But when the offer from the college came it was at the right moment. No interesting promotion was going to come my way for two or three years. I was on my own by then and felt restless. I had launched the three of you: Fred in the army, Richard in insurance and you in business. I thought I could well afford it.'

John frowned.

'But these sales of capital will affect your income quite a lot, at least for the time being?'

'Of course. I have taken the precaution of postponing the purchase of a new car, for which I was due, and also of cancelling a three-week tour of South Africa in January which I had planned. We shall go instead together to inspect your property in Berry . . .'

The Provost looked out of the window on the street, where a car had parked noisily.

'Good Heavens, there are Richard and Sue, and Paul,' he said. 'Why on earth couldn't they have let me know they were coming? Never mind. Stay here, please, John, and get some glasses out. And as you value our agreement, be civil to them. I will go and let them in.'

In a few moments there were voices in the entrance hall.

'Terribly sorry to take you by surprise, J.E. Sue and I each thought the other had telephoned. We are on our way to take Paul to school. We couldn't resist looking in on you. Hope it's not too inconvenient.'

'I have John staying with me,' said the Provost.

'Oh, John who?'

'Your brother John.'

'What? *John?*'

'Yes, he's been overworking. So he's come down here to have a bit of a holiday.'

And before there could be any reply the Provost brought them into the study.

'Sue, my dear, you remember John? It must be quite a long time since you have met. Paul, this is your uncle John.'

John was unaware of being anybody's uncle.

But the boy, introduced thus by the Provost, said quite unselfconsciously, as he shook hands, 'How do you do, Uncle John.'

Then it was Richard.

The brothers eyed each other with distaste, and exchanged a guarded 'Hello'.

The Provost brought out the drinks.

21

'What will you have, my dear?'

'Oh, a soft drink, for me, please, J.E. I am driving. And for Paul, of course. I'm sure Dick will have some your delicious sherry.'

John looked at his sister-in-law. He had not seen her since the wedding, which, he remembered, had been a simple blessing in church, as she was divorced. That ceremony was in fact the last family occasion he had attended. She was tall, dark and shapely – rather plain, intelligent-looking, well turned out and well made up, in a slightly over-ostentatious way. They viewed each other with a certain curiosity.

Then the Provost said, 'John, please find a soft drink. Greenfield won't be here yet.'

The pantry, into which John ventured for the first time, was well-provided. He returned with orange juice and tumblers and, having served Sue, and his nephew, who was talking excitedly to J.E., helped himself to sherry, and sat down beside Sue.

She tackled him boldly.

'Dick has always told me that you're the black sheep of the family. But you're not black and you don't look in the least sheepish. What have you been up to?'

Always more indulgent to the opposite sex, John decided that the impertinence was quite amusing and not unfriendly.

'I have been too busy making money, I'm afraid, to attend properly to my family.'

'Making money? That sounds promising. The Stock Exchange, is it?'

'Partly, but I'm also interested on my own in house property.'

'What sort of thing?'

'I look out for nice houses which have gone derelict and do them up. It is quite fun.'

'These are houses on the outskirts of London?'

'Within reach of London, yes.'

'How did you start?'

'A young couple I know were lamenting that they had fallen in love with just such a house, but all the contractors

22

they approached were going to take too long and charge too much. I said I'd see what I could do . . .'

'Sue, I think we ought to be on our way,' said Richard. 'Glad to see you looking so well, J.E. I hope you're not going to have too strenuous a term. Come, Paul . . .'

The Provost saw them out. At the window, John saw them getting into the car and heard Sue's somewhat brassy voice saying, 'But John's *nice*. Why haven't I been allowed to meet him before?'

He did not hear Richard's answer.

The Provost returned to the study.

'Have I got lipstick on my face, John? No? Good. I can't think why that dear woman has to put on all that warpaint. Bad as Serena Smith.'

John winced. He had not felt in any way committed to Serena and her two or three predecessors, nor expected them to feel committed to him, but he was still vexed to remember how easily she had been induced to leave him. Unexpectedly, his father was contrite.

'I'm sorry, John. I didn't know that was a sore subject. I didn't mean to hurt you.'

'But Sue? She's as common as dirt. Just like Richard to be so stupid. How did he come to strike up with her? Do you know?'

'Oh, yes. It's very simple. A shared interest in ballroom dancing.'

'Is Richard interested in ballroom dancing?'

'Passionately. All of you were taught to dance – your mother quite rightly insisted on that – but Richard became keen and when he got his first job he joined the local club. He met Sue there. She was a star, could have been professional, I gather. But a bit too tall. She was working in a bank when they met. Richard fell in love with her and that was that. I invited them my first year here for a college dance. They made quite a sensation.'

'A college dance? Did you take part yourself?'

'The dance committee wished me to open the ball. So I asked Sue. I should have been alarmed if I had known quite

23

how expert she was. She and Richard dance every week. I only knew that she was the most delightful person to partner I had ever danced with, except your mother.'

'Isn't Richard jealous of her dancing with other men?'

'I don't think so. He's quite used to her being a divinity on the dance floor and proud of it. As she isn't a divinity anywhere else – at least in public,' the Provost smiled discreetly, 'he can afford to be tolerant. She is a good wife to him. As to being common, yes: my parents, in the language of their generation, would have said that she wasn't out of the top drawer. But Sue has the brains. Quite apart from her talent for dancing. Richard wasn't all that stupid. I have come to have a considerable respect for her. And liking. Nowadays I suppose most large middle-class families cover a wide social spectrum. Thank God, both your brothers are happy in their marriages, different as they are. And that reminds me. I must ring up Fred. I don't want him to hear from Richard that you are here. I should have told them before. We seem to have been so busy. Stay with me, John. You might as well hear the conversation.'

The Provost dialled.

'Fred? How are things? How is Mary? . . . Good. Richard and Sue have just been here, with Paul. Oh, in excellent form. They were taking Paul back to school. No, on the contrary. He seemed very pleased and excited . . . Oh, come, why should you be envious? Haven't you got three enchanting little girls? . . . My other bit of news is that I have got your brother John staying with me. Yes. *John.* He's been overdoing things a bit and needs a rest. So I've persuaded him to come here. We're rigging up a room for him – you know what a big house this is – so that he can as far as possible live his own life under my roof. I must ring off now. Hope to see you soon. Love to Mary. And many big kisses to the girls . . .'

At the end of the morning, Mrs Mace left word that the room was ready.

The Provost said, 'Come and see if it is all right.'

They went upstairs and opened the door. They were greeted by an overwhelming smell of polish. John looked round. The divan was now covered by a stylish throw with matching cushions. The new desk was installed by the window, with his portable electronic typewriter on it. The new chairs were in place. His watercolour of Montmartre, by an artist friend of Henri's, hung over the fireplace. One of the Provost's Persian rugs glowed on the floor. There was a fan heater, radio and television. Secretly, John was somewhat relieved.

'Not too bad for a prison cell.'

'I'm glad you're satisfied,' said his father. 'See that your things have been put away as you would wish.'

John slid back the doors of the built-in cupboards.

Inside, his clothes were drawn up with almost military precision, all facing left. Tails, morning coat and dinner jacket led off, followed by a wine-coloured velvet jacket for more informal party wear, then his town suits, his tweeds, his sports and summer things, his overcoat, raincoat and dressing gown, with his shoes arranged below. On the shelves, his pullovers and scarves, shirts, pyjamas and handkerchieves were neatly stacked. In the last section, his extensive collection of ties was carefully suspended on a tape, while the boxes containing his hats occupied the floor-space.

'You've trained Mrs Mace pretty well,' he commented.

'She's always done a bit of valeting. And I have managed to teach her a little more.'

As he turned away, John noticed a piece of paper on the desk. He picked it up. It was a note written in a rustic but determined handwriting. He read it aloud.

'Mr John. I hope as how everything is all right. Your bed will be made weekdays while you has breakfast. Leave any washing you wants done on the bed. The room will be turned out Mondays 9.00 to 10.00.'

The last words were underlined twice.

'Which means: don't dare to try to use the room yourself during that hour', explained the Provost.

'You are not the only autocrat in the Lodgings, then?'

'She is one of the most obstinate women I have ever known. She has worked for at least two Provosts before me, so they are small beer to her. But she does the work well. I advise making a point of thanking her tomorrow. They must have worked hard to get the room ready.' And the Provost added, as they came downstairs, 'By the way, you will need some papers, won't you? *The Financial Times,* for instance? What else? *The Economist?* Let me know. And don't forget to renew your reader's ticket for the university library.'

2

For the next few days there were regular consultations about
money. The letters which arose from them, and from his
dealings with France, were mostly typed by John and checked
with his father before dispatch and they studied the
incoming letters together. This seemed natural, in the circumstances. Then an envelope arrived on the breakfast
table, addressed to John, which was evidently something
different. It was handwritten and bore a local postmark. He
opened it. It was from the wife of Dr Fletcher and contained
an invitation to a sherry party.

He started when his father said, 'May I see?' but pushed
the letter over to him. The Provost read it with a smile. 'You
must have made a good impression on Clive. Would you
like to go? You can accept any invitation from fellows of the
college.'

John was cautious.

'I suppose it will be frightfully dull.'

'If a party is dull, it is usually as much the fault of the
guests as the hosts,' commented the Provost.

'She says it's for their daughter Pamela, who is going to
be home for the weekend. What's the girl like?'

'Pleasant enough. She is a physiotherapist in London.'

'I think I'll go.'

Back in his room, John wrote a note of acceptance. Downstairs, he found the Provost in his study.

'I've written to Mrs Fletcher. Can I have a stamp?'

His father looked up.

'May I see what you have written?'

27

Annoyed, John said, 'I've done up the envelope now.'

'I'm afraid you will have to undo it, then.'

'But that's absurd. You know what I have said.'

'All the same, I would like to see the letter.'

'But this is a fuss about nothing. It's so trivial.'

'It's not trivial. Either you show me all your letters, incoming and outgoing, or our agreement is cancelled and you will have to fend for yourself.'

It became clear the Provost was in earnest. By that time he realized that he would have done better to give in gracefully at the beginning, but he had worked himself into such a paroxysm of rage that he could see no way out.

Then the Provost went over to his desk, picked up a small paperknife and handed it to his son, saying, as coolly as if he had been asking someone to pass the butter at table,

'Please open the letter, John.'

In silence, he took it, slit open the envelope, and surrendered the letter.

'That's fine,' said his father, having glanced at it. 'I had quite forgotten what a nice handwriting you have. You will find stamps in the top right-hand drawer of my desk.'

John began the next day in a better mood. He had swum before breakfast for the first time at his new abode and enjoyed himself so much that he was a little late joining his father. He found two letters waiting for him. One was from France, acknowledging receipt of a payment. The other was from Miranda Elton, inviting him to an evening party at her flat. It was agreed that he should go.

While the Provost was with his secretary, he went up to his room, taking with him the newspapers and Miranda's letter. He sat down and wrote to her accepting. Then he paused.

It was in itself unimportant whether anyone else saw the contents of his note. They were, as he said to himself, innocuous to the point of inanity. But the prospect of submitting them to his father under compulsion was extremely disagreeable, after his searing encounter the previous day. He had been spared a reminder of the obligation to show his answer. Nonetheless, it seemed unavoidable. Could he, at least, devise some face-saving manoeuvre? He had been told to play a part. Why not perform as if he were acting of his own free will?

He came downstairs, and, finding his father alone, said with studied casualness, 'Would you mind having a look at what I have said to Miranda Elton? I have no experience of writing to women fellows of the college and I don't want to blot my copybook.'

'I'm sure what you have written is just right, John', responded the Provost at once. 'But of course I will look at it for you.'

He handed back the letter approvingly.

'No lady, academic or otherwise, could fail to be pleased with such a reply.'

Henceforth some variant on this ritual took place over each of John's private letters. It was a rather sour little piece of domestic comedy. But it served its purpose. It distanced the act of compliance from the threat of sanctions.

And the Provost, on his side began, quite naturally and unobtrusively, to show him some of his own personal correspondence.

'Quite a good effort for a six-year-old, don't you think?'

This was a thank-you note from one of Fred's daughters after her birthday. It began, 'Dear Granddad . . .'

John was surprised. He had hardly thought of J.E. as a grandfather.

'Oh, one acquires so many different identities,' said the Provost. 'One gets used to it. I remember years ago the little shock I felt on being introduced to someone as "Una's fiancé . . ."'

A few days later another identity revealed itself. A letter from a woman professor in the United States began, 'Dear Jimmy . . .'

'She is an old friend, Francesca Melzi, who has had a chair in America for a number of years,' explained the Provost. 'And she tells me, as you see, that she is going to take early retirement and return to live in London.'

'But I thought no one addressed you as "Jimmy" except Mama.'

'She was a childhood friend of your mother's – they were an Italian family who had settled in England – and I suppose she had always heard me called "Jimmy", just as I always knew her as "Fanny". I have seen her only occasionally since she went to the States, though we have always kept in touch. She is an art historian: I believe, now a rather eminent one. I'll tip off Bob Rogers – he's the professor of Fine Art here – and suggest securing her to talk to one of his seminars or give a lecture, in due course.'

Always adaptable, John was beginning to adjust himself to the new conditions and to feel almost at home in the Lodgings. At one point it threatened to create an illusion of freedom. Finding that he needed to consult a periodical which he did not have handy, he bethought himself of the Provost's advice to renew his membership of the university library and ran out at once to do so. It took quite a long time. He had to have a photograph taken for the new ticket, which involved waiting in a queue. Then he had to find his way to the relevant reading-room and track down the article he wanted. When he returned, the Provost was sitting down to lunch.

He waited until Greenfield had left the room, and then asked, 'Wherever have you been all this time?'

John told him.

'Why didn't you say at breakfast that you were going to do this?'

'I hadn't thought of it then.'

'Then you should have left me a note.'

John had completely forgotten this formality, and said so.

'Really?' There was a pause. 'Let me see your reader's ticket, please.'

John bridled.

'You think I was doing something else? Something nefarious, I suppose.'

'No. I think you are probably telling the truth. But I want proof. I can't afford to take any chances.'

Grudgingly, John took out his wallet and extracted the ticket. His father looked at it and gave it back to him.

'All right. But be more careful another time . . .'

If it had been his intention to perpetrate any deceit, he now realized that it would have been hard to carry it out, with every letter and every financial transaction open to inspection, every movement monitored and no independent access to a telephone. He was effectively caged. But, ever resilient, he recognized that the cage was roomy and comfortable, even luxurious in some respects. If through impatience and carelessness he bumped into the unseen bars, he got hurt, not otherwise. And from then on relations with his father became, as he said to himself, 'less adversarial'. He had braced himself for recriminations about the long period of their estrangement. There were none. By tacit mutual consent, it was never mentioned. He was always treated with a certain courtesy, even at moments of tension. And increasingly the Provost made moves which, to an outsider, might have seemed friendly.

'I'm free this afternoon until five, when I have a committee meeting. What about an outing to the country? Caneyfield House, perhaps? The gardens ought to be looking nice now. And would you like to try the Rover? I've arranged with the insurance for you to be able to drive it.'

Another day, when a dinner guest had been obliged to cancel, 'Shall we go to the theatre? There's a new play on. I don't know anything about it, or about the cast. You probably do. Or there's a concert of baroque music, mostly Telemann. Quite a good group. Authentic instruments, so-called. Here are the details, in the local press. You choose.'

In these cases it was clear that the Provost would not go unless he did. John could hardly imagine that his company was indispensable to his father's pleasure. Rather, he supposed, he was not going to be left to his own devices at the Lodgings. But he accepted.

31

A little later, he read about an exhibition at Burlington House which attracted him.

'But I suppose I'm not allowed to go to London by myself?'

'Not yet, John. But let me see the review. It sounds good, doesn't it? Pictures from private collections. Why don't we go together? We could go up by an early train, see the exhibition before it gets too crowded, and have lunch at the club.'

John was deliberately surly.

'I suppose that would be better than not going at all.'

The Provost was already consulting his diary.

'Friday looks possible. I'll ring up and book a table.'

Though their tastes in art were by no means identical, they both went round the exhibition with interest. They were still talking about it when they crossed Piccadilly and began to make their way to the club. John reminded his father that the first art exhibition he had ever been to was at Burlington House.

'Mama bought me a catalogue for myself, wrote my name and the date on the cover, and showed me how to use it. I've still got it. The brothers were bored stiff. Serve them right. *I* was always being dragged off to idiotic films and rotten football matches that *they* wanted to see.'

The Provost corrected his memories.

'Not quite *always*. I remember one occasion when you utterly refused to come with them and me on some excursion of that kind. You yelled, "I don't *want* to go" and shouted and stamped until you were purple in the face. You wanted to stay with Mama, but she was committed to going on a shopping expedition and meeting friends at the Savoy for tea. You were too big to be taken off against your will and too small to be left at home. In the end she agreed, with much misgiving, to take you with her. Afterwards she told me you had been "a little angel", sat up while she tried on endless dresses and hats at different shops, offering very pertinent comments on each, carried all her parcels without being asked, opened doors for her, remembered at tea to pass the cakes and not to interrupt, and were pronounced by her friends to be "such a *dear* little boy and *so* well behaved". And your mother couldn't help laughing . . . I don't expect you remember that.'

'I only remember having a wonderful afternoon with Mama. All those lovely clothes and silly hats – smart pretty ladies, none so pretty and smart as her – gorgeous cakes – jolly view of the river . . .'

Less agreeable recollections presented themselves as they approached the portals of the club. He had been taken there occasionally as a boy. There was no place where he had felt more hopelessly in his father's shadow. When he embarked on his career, J.E. had offered to put him up for membership and to pay the entrance fee and the first year's subscription. He had refused.

'Stuffy old place. All male. Hasn't even got a swimming pool.'

He looked round now with grudging admiration at the stately dining room and wondered whether there was going to be any allusion to that episode.

But his father was absorbed in the menu.

'What would you like to start with? *Hors d'oeuvre?* Right. And what for the main course? Dover sole? I shall have that too.' He wrote their choices down and gave them to the waitress. 'Let's look at the wine list. They have an excellent Meursault. Would you like that? Good. We'll have a bottle.'

After lunch they moved to another room for coffee.

Almost at once, a man who was already sitting there got up and came over to speak to them. His face was familiar, probably from television appearances, and John seemed to remember that he had been a junior minister in a previous government.

'J.E., how nice to see you. May I join you?'

John was introduced. Then the politician noticed the catalogue of the exhibition, which was lying on their table.

'How did you find the pictures? I was at the opening last week, but I hadn't time to stay long.'

'I enjoyed them – most of them. But you must ask John.

33

He's the nearest approach to an art connoisseur in the family . . .'

Back at the Lodgings, John began to experiment with acting as a dutiful member of the household, answering the door when Greenfield was not there. He found it quite amusing. Over a basic routine of meals and meetings which had probably changed little since Edwardian times, there were unpredictable variations.

His first visitor was a chemistry student about to begin his second year, who was panting with indignation because the tutor in Slavonic studies would not let him change his course to Russian. The tutors were all such pedants. The Provost was a man of the world; he would take his part. He didn't. But he gave the young man nearly an hour of his time.

'Absurd, of course. But it all came out: he has recently acquired a Russian girlfriend. *Cherchez la femme* . . . I think I have convinced him that the best thing he could do – for both of them – is to get a good degree in chemistry.'

Not all the little dramas were internal ones.

An Australian professor on sabbatical leave, who was an old member of the college, called one evening, after having made a relatively brief courtesy visit earlier in the day: he had missed the last train to Manchester, and all the local hotels were full, so could the Provost find him a bed for the night?

An elegant American lady arrived asking to see a portrait of her great-great-grandfather which was said to be in St Matthew's.

The police turned up, having failed to locate the dean, about an unfortunate student who had been robbed coming back to his lodgings the previous night.

Reporters descended on the college when an old member, a colourful politician, was suddenly found to be at the centre of a promising scandal . . .

And, as the term approached, university and college friends and colleagues tended to drop in for a chat.

On one occasion, returning from the library, John opened

34

the door of the study to find the Provost drinking sherry with an oldish man whom he did not recognize.

He had expressly been told not to knock, but he murmured an apology and was about to withdraw, when J.E. called out, 'Don't run away, John. Come in.' He was introduced. 'This is my son John, who is staying with me. John, – the vice-chancellor.'

Deciding that the visitor looked benevolent, John said, as he shook hands, 'I beg your pardon, sir: have I interrupted a conspiracy?'

'Oh, I hardly think you could dignify our gossip with such a name, eh, J.E.?'

'We were just talking over some items of business which will soon be coming up. Get a glass and give yourself some sherry, John. One of the items might interest you. It is trying to make better provision for swimming: a proper swimming pool, in fact.'

'That would be marvellous, but enormously expensive, I suppose? If you mean a full-sized 50-metre pool?'

'That's the trouble. We may yet ask you to twist the arm of some of your wealthy friends in the City.'

They talked for a short time about sport. Then the vice-chancellor got up to go.

'Stay for lunch with us, Alan,' said the Provost.

'No, thank you very much. You're always so hospitable. But I must be on my way.'

John saw him to the door.

'Your father still plays a very good game of tennis,' he observed. 'That is to say, he usually beats me. Nice to meet you, John.'

And he ambled out.

John began to view his position more dispassionately. He told himself that the present régime, with all its disagreeable and unreasonable constraints, was the price he had to pay for being rescued from disaster and that it would only last for a few months more. To sulk was not in his nature. He had always aimed at getting the most fun he could out of any situation and, although the opportunities for that at present were limited, he began to work out a strategy for exploiting them. To cultivate an active social life of his own, even though it had to begin with his father's circle of colleagues and friends, seemed the most promising approach.

The Fletchers' party gave him his first opportunity. He wondered, as he drove there, how he would get on, as he expected to know only his host.

He was reassured when the vice-provost, who had clearly been on the lookout for him, came to the door at once to welcome him, saying, 'Come and meet my wife. Barbara, this is John Egerton.'

Mrs Fletcher was nothing if not a good hostess, though she had the disconcerting habit of looking over your shoulder to mark down the next person she meant to talk to. He was promptly introduced to their daughter, Pamela, and to several fellow guests. He consciously exerted himself to be agreeable, but ended up by really enjoying himself. When he judged it time to leave, Dr Fletcher came out with him.

'Oh, ho – the Provost's Rover? The apple of his eye? He must have great confidence in you.'

'He's so indulgent,' said John, unctuously . . .

The Rover was not available for Miranda Elton's party. The Provost would not be back in time from a meeting the other side of the town. But her flat, though some distance away in a northern suburb, was on a main bus route and the buses ran until 11 o'clock. He went over the plan carefully with his father.

'I ought to be able to leave between 10.30 and 10.45. Allowing say half an hour for the bus trip, I should be back by 11.30. Will that be OK?'

'Right. 11.30 it shall be.'

He dressed with special care, putting on his wine-coloured jacket, black trousers, a dashing tie, and he took a raincoat as the weather was threatening. He set off, caught the bus, and walked the short distance to Miranda's upstairs flat. The party was highly congenial. He collected an invitation to

36

review a forthcoming production of *The Family Reunion* at another college. He stayed a long time. The drinks circulated briskly and the party was clearly set to continue at least until midnight. Suddenly he realized that it must be time to go. He extricated himself as quickly as he decently could, ran downstairs and, as it had begun to rain, put on his waterproof before going out. He hurried down the street towards the bus stop. The bus was just disappearing in the distance. He looked at his watch. It was 11.05. He could hardly return to Miranda's and beg a lift. He saw a callbox a short distance further on and decided to try to get a taxi. But he had not much hope of finding one on a wet night and, in fact, none of the offices replied. He would have to walk. At least, he thought, he could warn the Provost that he would be late. He dialled the Lodgings.

'J.E., I'm terribly sorry. I was a bit late leaving Miranda's party and I've just missed the last bus. I can't get a taxi. I shall walk. I suppose it'll take me about an hour.'

The Provost wasted no time on reproaches.

'Where are you speaking from?' he asked.

'A callbox on the corner of Boyle Street.'

'Right. Stay where you are. I'll come and fetch you. For Heaven's sake don't walk. Wait for me. I shall have to get the car out again.'

He rang off. Some ten minutes later, John saw through the rain the dipped headlights and the dim shape of a big car slowing down on the other side of the road. It made a U-turn and drew up beside the telephone box. The passenger door opened.

'Jump in.'

'This is awfully kind of you, J.E.,' murmured John, as he scrambled in. 'I could have walked.'

'You would have been extremely late and extremely wet. And some of the streets nearer the town centre are not safe at this time of night. I know you're young and strong, but there might be three or four of these thugs.'

They drove back in silence. Safely at the Lodgings, John anticipated a tremendous row.

He said, 'I really am sorry. You must be angry.'

'Of course I'm angry. What gentleman in England wouldn't be angry at having to turn out at this hour to fetch a son because he's missed the last bus home? But at least you had the sense to ring up. You wouldn't have been here until 12.30 if you had walked and I would have been worried that you had been in an accident. Now let's go to bed. The beginning of term is almost upon us, and I have a meeting of the governing body tomorrow – or rather, as it's already past midnight, this afternoon.'

The next day, the Provost explained the routine on Sundays in term.

'I ask five or six of the first year to lunch. I don't expect they enjoy it much, but at least they get a good meal and I get to know them. You'll help me to entertain them.'

'All right. Do you want me to look up beforehand who they are?'

'Don't bother. It will give you something to talk about.'

'What shall I wear?'

'Anything you like. I know you are always smart. *They* don't dress up. Mostly they come in jeans.'

'Jeans for lunch with the Provost?'

'Some of them haven't anything else. Students are often extremely hard up these days. And those who aren't like to pretend they are. Some of the girls try to dress up, sometimes with strange results: miniskirts and fancy leggings, or skirts sweeping the floor, with great clod-hopping boots. Or even bare feet.'

John did his best. But the girls, on this occasion at least, were, in his estimation, all either drabs or frumps. And, although some of them at least seemed genuinely keen on the course they had undertaken, others had little idea of conversation except complaining about their expenses – 'whingeing' as he termed it – and their attempts to please him fell flat.

It was small consolation to hear the Provost say, tolerantly,

'The first Sunday of this term tends to be the stickiest party. The poor things don't even know each other yet.'

To add to his disgust, he found that he was expected to attend the evening service in chapel. He knew that his father was "religious", if only because on Sundays they had breakfast later to allow time for him to return from church. Hitherto he himself had not been involved. He voiced his opposition, cautiously. He had become circumspect about provoking outright confrontation.

'But you haven't insisted until now, J.E.'

'Sunday morning is a communion service. It would be quite improper for me to force you to come to that. College chapel is another thing.'

With dismal recollections of school chapel, John persisted.

'It would be quite meaningless to me, in fact sheer hypocrisy. Surely you don't want my act to extend to pretending piety?'

'No need for devoutness. Just behave with decorum. The chapel is part of the routine of the college. It is a cross-section, though admittedly nowadays a small one, of college society.'

'I don't *want* to meet the sort of college society which goes to chapel.'

'How do you know? You haven't come across them yet.'

The Provost's tone showed that he meant business. John sighed.

'All right. I'll come quietly. But under protest. Do I go in with you, or what?'

'We'll walk over together. The chaplain will be there waiting for me. You have met him. So you should say "Good evening", or just "Hello" if you prefer. Then go in and find yourself a seat. I come in then with the chaplain.'

The college chapel was a small, plain late seventeenth-century building. The college's poverty, he saw, had at least saved it from being modernized to suit more recent tastes, or even demolished and rebuilt, as had happened in some other institutions. As he expected, he found the proceedings there exceedingly dull. He sought what amusement he could find in studying the congregation. The centre lights were too dim to see people clearly. But he saw two girls seated next to each other who seemed older and smarter than the average undergraduate. One was dark, with well-cut short hair, wearing glasses, and dressed in a black jacket and trousers. The other was fair and looked pretty as far as he could see, with wavy hair falling on her shoulders, wearing a loose pink tunic over a quite long pale blue skirt. He made a mental note to ask the Provost who they were.

As he came out of chapel, a polite voice behind him said, 'Good evening, Mr Egerton.'

He turned, and saw the smiling face of the Jamaican whom he had met the first night at dinner.

'Good evening, Dr Sopes. And my name is John.'

'And mine is Jonathan.'

Surprised at finding him there, John could not resist asking, 'Do many people in your country go to church?'

'Oh, yes,' replied Jonathan. 'We have two religions and we take both mighty seriously.'

'Two religions?'

'Oh, yes. Christianity and cricket.'

'I see. At any rate, you can practise both all the year round.'

By this time they were outside in the quadrangle.

'Will you be here next Sunday, John? If so, would you by any chance be free after chapel? I am having a few friends for drinks and some sort of supper in my rooms. Could you join us?'

'A Caribbean party?' said the Provost, when told. 'It will probably go on all night. At least it's in college, so you can be as late as you like. I'm sure you will be in good hands. And you will get out of having to dine with the bishop and me.'

'What bishop?'

'You didn't listen to the notices. But why should you? He is an old member of the college, an honorary fellow, who is going to preach next Sunday. It will be a better sermon than the one perpetrated this week by the chaplain. He is

40

a good young man, and good with the students, but a poor performer in the pulpit.'

John not only escaped dinner with the bishop. He had a most exhilarating evening.

He was introduced as 'John Egerton, who knows all about investments.'

'Does anybody?' he protested and in high good humour he launched out with them into animated discussion on the world economy. The company was composed mainly, but not exclusively, of West Indians. One of them went to help Jonathan when he withdrew to his small kitchen to prepare 'some sort of supper'. It was then already well after 8.30. But he emerged barely three-quarters of an hour later, bringing in a trolley loaded with sumptuous exotic dishes. Disposable knives, forks and spoons, plates and napkins were expertly distributed. While they ate, jazz began to play softly in the background. Then the conversation redoubled. It was long after midnight when the party broke up. John had appreciated particularly the pleasure of meeting people as clever as himself. He tended to see only those with financial skills, in his London routine. It reminded him of the shock he had experienced in his first term at the university, which had quickly turned to enjoyment as he pitted his wits against brilliant contemporaries. And before he left, he had been invited to address an informal group, to which most of them belonged, which met two or three times a term.

'Whatever topic you like. Could be The London Stock Exchange, could be the UK housing market . . .'

He was gratified, but a little alarmed.

'I did economics, with history, for my degree course. But I've forgotten it all.'

'Probably just as well,' said another of Jonathan's guests, reassuringly. 'What you learnt then is sure to be out of date now. What we should be interested in is, how it looks from the inside.'

'I think I could manage that. Next term, perhaps?' said John.

*   *   *

But he had not forgotten to ask the Provost about the two girls he had observed in chapel.

'Oh, I know who you mean,' said his father, at once. 'The brunette is Emily Wilkinson. She got a good degree in law here and is now doing a course in European law. The blonde is Amanda Orson. She did French and Italian at her home university and is taking the diploma in fine art here. They share a flat.'

'Would it be possible for me to meet them?'

'Nothing easier. I am giving a party for the graduates next week. They are both coming.'

With much less pleasure, John learnt that there had been a phone call from Richard: he had to visit a client in the neighbourhood in a few days' time and asked whether he could take the chance of calling in. The Provost had agreed the following Thursday and had invited him to lunch.

'Oh, Hell,' said John, grumpily. 'Won't there even be that dear woman, as you call her – Sue, isn't she? Undiluted Richard? No. I'd rather have no lunch at all.'

'That's out of the question,' replied the Provost. 'It would look very strange if we three did not have lunch together. But he is coming at 12.30 and I should be happy to see him on his own then. You needn't join us until a little before 1 o'clock. I'll say you are at the library.'

'I shan't have anything to say to him.'

'Yes, you will. I've thought up a scenario.'

'A scenario?'

'Something short of lines for you to speak, as we don't know what Richard will say. But a rough plan. Like this: when you come in he and I will be having drinks together. You will say "Hello". It needn't be cordial, but it mustn't be hostile. Then you will say, "How is Sue?" Not too solici-tously. Just politely. Then, if there is a pause, you will ask how Paul is getting on at school.'

'Will he really suppose that I am interested in hearing how his brat is getting on at school?'

'Probably not. Just ask it as a courtesy. I am sure he will take it as such. Then I will try to steer the conversation on to the prospects for the general election. He knows a bit about politics – is on the committee of the local Conservative association. That ought to be a useful topic and reasonably safe, don't you think?'

John acquitted himself tolerably well in a part which he assumed most unwillingly.

He hoped that the graduate party would at least be a little more amusing.

He made a point of arriving early and quickly got into discussion with a keen historian who was beginning a thesis on the French Revolution in an area not far from Berry. The young man was just warming to his subject when he suddenly broke off and stared.

'Good Heavens!' he exclaimed. 'Have we got a film star among us?'

John turned to see what he was looking at. It was Amanda Orson, who had just come into the room with Emily Wilkinson. She was not just pretty. She was breathtaking.

Theirs was not the only conversation which had come to an abrupt halt.

Without any apparent awareness of the sensation she was making, she went up to the Provost and returned his greeting with a shy smile. He promptly motioned John and his companion to come forward and introduced them to her and Emily, before moving to receive other guests. Her face at once became grave again. She proved to be a pleasant, even accomplished conversationalist. But there was something withdrawn about her which nettled him. Conscious, as he could hardly fail to be, of possessing good looks, beautiful manners and not inconsiderable charm, he was used to finding a positive response in most of the women he met. If there was no flirtatiousness, there was normally at least a smile. He got one from Emily. But Amanda, as she talked to him, did not flutter an eyelash. She was calm, composed, slightly appraising. The look was not insolent, but the marvellous cornflower blue eyes remained chilly. Then another man came up, who evidently knew her already. She was no more forthcoming to him. He succeeded however in bearing her off on the pretext of introducing her to someone else. John was left with Emily, as the historian had drifted away in Amanda's direction. He found her good company. She was nice-looking, without being in the same class as her flatmate, and she talked readily about her plans and about her boyfriend, who was a year ahead of her in law and already had a pupillage in London.

After the party, he spoke to the Provost about the impression that Amanda Orson had made on him.

'Yes,' said his father. 'She's an uncommonly handsome woman, and, with it, unusually reserved, though I do not find her in the least dull.'

'I notice that she wears a wedding ring. Is there a jealous husband in the offing?'

'No, no. She is a widow. The poor chap was killed in the Gulf War – or officially "missing believed killed". He was an RAF pilot.'

'That's years ago.'

'Well, she told me when I interviewed her that she believes he still may be alive. And she was evidently very devoted to him. I am not quite sure why she told me that, but I *think* the message was, "So don't imagine please, Mr Provost, that I want to come here to choose another husband." I certainly didn't imagine that. She is clearly dedicated to the subject.'

'What about the guy who claimed acquaintance with her? I didn't catch the name. Dark. Bearded. Wears spectacles. An art student, I gathered.'

'That would be Alban Miller. They must meet quite often. It's a small department. He's researching on Berthe Morisot.'

'Berthe Morisot? I like her paintings. But is there really anything new to say about her?'

'Bob Rogers, the professor, thinks that it's all right. Miller claims to have found unpublished material in France. His father is a wealthy man – he makes no secret of it – and has bought him some of it, and even a couple of the pictures.'

John looked curiously at his father.

'How do you know about all these people and what they are doing?'

'It is part of the job. And it interests me.'

'You have files on them, I suppose? And photographs?'

'Oh, yes, it's quite simple. There is only some memorizing to do. And it doesn't matter too much if one has an occasional lapse in talking to them, not like forgetting the name of another head of house, or of his wife – or her husband as the case may be. I once called the wife of the French Professor "Suzanne" instead of "Simone," not to her face, but in his hearing, and it took me a long time to live it down.'

'That side of it must be frightfully tedious. I suppose you have endless official entertaining and with a lot of boring people to meet.'

'I rarely find it tedious. Your mother and I used to entertain a good deal in London. She was brilliant at it. Without her, it isn't the same. Nothing is. But I still enjoy it. There are some academic bores, naturally. I don't find them worse than civil service bores, or political bores, or business bores – you must have come across some of *them*?'

The most notable of the Provost's social events that term was in fact the celebration of a biennial lecture, open to the public, named after General de Gaulle, which had been endowed by a rich and fervently francophile old member of the college. This time it was to be given by a veteran gaullist politician and he and his wife were to dine in the college after the lecture. Dinner for 20 guests, to include local professors of history and of French, the director of the French Institute, selected members of the French and History faculties, and fellows of the college, all with their respective wives or husbands. The vice-chancellor regretted that he was already booked for some function in London.

'And I get Barbara Fletcher to take the other end of the table on these occasions. She is very experienced. John, you

45

will be one of the guests, of course. Your French is fluent – or used to be – and it will come in useful.'

They looked at the list of acceptances with Mrs Macrae, who had already made the place-cards.

'I shall have Madame, the lecturer's wife, on my right and the professor's wife on my left. Mrs Fletcher will of course have the lecturer on her right; he's said to speak some English, and Barbara can certainly muster some French . . .' Finally almost all the table seating plan had been decided. 'That leaves you in the middle, next to the French wife of one of the faculty members. All right, John? Good.'

'It is going to be a black tie occasion, I take it?' John later asked.

'No, no,' said the Provost. 'The poor old lecturer wouldn't thank us for having to pack his *smoking* and in any case most people will come here more or less direct from the lecture, as it's at 6 o'clock. *Tenue de ville* is the order of the day for the gentlemen: your best dark suit in fact. Of course the ladies can wear what they please. And that reminds me that I shall have to explain to Madame the barbarous English custom of the men and women separating temporarily after dinner. It's not done in Scotland, John – the "auld alliance" has seen to that.'

'And how do you explain it?'

'I have always heard that most English gentlemen in the old days didn't think a dinner party complete without drinking themselves under the table and that the ladies were given the opportunity to flee the room before they began the process.'

'How will you explain this to Madame in French?' asked John.

'Good question. I am a bit rusty.' The Provost looked thoughtful. '*Si nous parlions un peu de français, mon fils?*'

'*Je veux bien, papa. Allons-y.*'

The Provost began to translate into French his remarks on English dinner customs. He was good, but slow and careful. John was in much better practice. He was only stumped

46

for finding an equivalent for the expression 'to drink them-selves under the table'. The dictionary did not seem to offer a solution . . .

But the result was evidently highly successful. At the dinner, John looked up the table for a moment to the Prov-ost over the brilliantly candlelit table, glittering with silver, and it was apparent that Madame, who had sat through her husband's lecture with dignified resignation, was now having a very good time indeed. He himself had delightful com-pany. Then the moment came for the ladies to leave the room. Mrs Fletcher, having received the Provost's discreet message from the butler, rose, caught the eye of the women guests, and duly led them out.

The Provost assembled the men at his end of the table, and said, 'Drink up your port, gentlemen, and we will join the ladies in five minutes . . .'

As the last guests left, Mrs Fletcher turned to John with a smile and said, 'What a successful party. These occasions can be very stiff and formal. But your father is such a splen-did host . . .'

'And now,' said the Provost next morning, 'you had better go and exercise your French in a more prosaic cause. Don't you think it is time you went and inspected your property in Berry?'

'I should like nothing better,' replied John. 'Shall I tele-phone the contractors? And the hotel?'

'Go ahead. As soon as you have arranged your meetings, Mrs Macrae will book your flight and arrange for a Hertz car to be at Charles de Gaulle airport for you. Will you drive all the way in one day?'

John nodded.

'It's only 240 kilometres and I know the road well. Just ask Mrs Macrae to be sure to get me a good car. I have sometimes broken the journey with Henri and Chantal at Orleans; I can easily go direct.' He paused, disconcerted by the unexpected prospect of temporary freedom. 'Any conditions, J.E.?'

'Only to telephone me to tell me how you have got on. You'll be away two nights, I expect? Don't hurry it . . .'

John stopped in Bourges in the late afternoon for an appointment with Maître Cadenet, who took a more cheerful view of his affairs than he, having had no idea of the financial crisis which had loomed.

'They take their time, of course. It is annoying. I know you had hoped to have the replacement for the *château* completed by now. It is always the way if one is not after them constantly. I have been over occasionally. But they are more afraid of you. You know too much about their job for their liking.'

He drove the few miles further to the village, arriving at the *Hôtel du Château* in time for dinner. He rang up his father before going to bed.

The next day he drove early to the park and went over the site with the workmen when they arrived. The work had been well carried out, on the whole, but he was far from satisfied with the pace at which it was proceeding. When the contractors turned up, he told them so in no uncertain terms.

'I want to be able to show the house to prospective buyers early in the new year,' he said, peremptorily. 'Not necessarily finished, but with the roof on.'

'But, Monsieur, the winter is coming on. The weather . . .'

'All the more reason to get a move on.'

He spent the rest of the day on the site, and made a lot of notes, of which he gave a copy to the foreman. It was dusk when he returned to the hotel. He rang up his father, glanced at the newspaper and then went in to dinner.

He was well looked after by the same waiter as the previous evening. But this time a waitress had come on duty on the further side of the dining room. She came over to him, and said,

'*Bon soir, Monsieur. Vous allez bien?*'

Accustomed by now to being recognized by the staff of the hotel, he acknowledged her greeting absent-mindedly.

But she kept hovering round him whenever she had a spare moment.

Finally, when he was finishing his coffee, she asked, '*Monsieur désire encore quelque chose?*'

He looked up, slightly irritated. She was quite pretty. It came back to him that, on one of his previous visits, he had flirted with her, at least mildly.

Gallantly, he managed to raise a smile, but said, firmly, '*Non, merci. Je suis servi. Bon soir, Mademoiselle. Bonne nuit.*'

She withdrew, disconsolate.

After watching the TV news, he sat down in his room with the local newspaper. He found himself wondering why he no longer felt the slightest interest in the waitress. He had difficulty even in remembering what she looked like. Then a quite different image floated into his mind. It was Amanda Orson. After a moment, he shook off the impression and went back to his paper. But the image came back.

He was puzzled. Apart from the brief encounter at the Provost's party, he had hardly seen her. The first Sunday after, he had made a point of timing his exit from the chapel to coincide with Amanda and Emily and greeting them. They had both replied politely and, after a few moments, moved away.

He had tended to dismiss her as a haughty beauty. But why did a picture of her intervene when he thought of another pretty girl? He made up his mind that he must see more of her.

He had asked Jonathan Sopes, and other of the younger fellows with whom he had become friendly, to drinks *tête à tête* in his room. He could not see Amanda responding to that sort of invitation. But perhaps, if he invited other people as well, including her friend Emily, that might lead to better acquaintance?

Accordingly, on his return he said to his father, 'Do you think I might give a small party? I have had so much hospitality from people here. And there are some members of the college whom I would like to get to know better.'

'Why not?' said the Provost, at once. 'What have you in

mind? A sherry party? Or a buffet supper? You can have the parlour any day that I am not using it.'

'I was really proposing to have drinks in my room.'

'Of course. It would be more your own thing, as the young say. I take it none of your guests would object to climbing two flights of stairs? That is quite common in colleges, after all. How many people would you invite?'

'I suppose 12 or 14.'

'It sounds rather a squash. But I forgot: you're used to entertaining in a London flat.'

'Yes. I had probably better stick to 12. Besides, there's ourselves.'

'You don't have to ask me.'

'It would look strange if you weren't there. As if you were boycotting the proceedings.'

'As you wish. I could look in say for half an hour on my way over to dinner in Hall.'

Diaries were consulted. A date was chosen.

'Good. I'll start writing the invitations,' said John. Then he paused. 'I suppose you will want to see them?'

'No,' replied his father, unexpectedly. 'In fact, that rule has served its purpose. From now onwards, show me your letters if you want to, not otherwise.'

In the end they drew up the list together. John had come to have a healthy respect for the Provost's social skills and sought his advice.

'Pamela Fletcher? She might be at home as it's on a Saturday. Will she know all the St Matthew's people?'

'Not necessarily. Probably not the graduates, if you are planning to invite any of them. You will have to do some introducing. Can you manage that as well as the drinks, or would you like someone to help with serving?'

'I think I can manage. I will make a plan, as I have seen you do, of who should be introduced to whom, and memorize it. Yes, I did think of inviting a few of the graduates. Amanda Orson and Emily Wilkinson, and I might as well as Alban Miller – he seems quite a civilized man. Jonathan, of course, and a couple of his friends. Miranda Elton . . .'

They looked critically at the final draft.

'That's quite a good mix of subjects. And of the sexes, if you count us,' commented the Provost. 'I'm glad you're having the two girls. They both work hard. Neither is well off. Their face is their fortune, but they are not the sort to capitalize on it. I suspect they don't get much fun.'

'I find Amanda rather fascinating,' admitted John.

'It would be hard for any young man of taste *not* to. But I hope you're not thinking of trying to recruit her as one of your playthings,' said the Provost.

'J.E.,' said John, with dignity, 'I shouldn't dream of recruiting any member of your college as a plaything. It would do neither of us any good. I am on my best behaviour here. And in any case, Amanda doesn't look the plaything sort. She would be more demanding than that, I fancy.'

At his party, she indeed looked more imposing than ever. She wore the same dress as for the graduate reception, enlivened only by a different necklace. But she had put up her hair. It was combed straight back and coiled into a solid chignon, tied round with a chiffon scarf which matched the dress. Not even the odd tendril relieved the severity. On her, this austere style served to set off to still better advantage the finely sculptured features, the graceful curve of the neck and the dainty ears.

She was a quiet but amiable guest. She looked with appreciation at his watercolour of Paris.

'I have a rather similar view of Montmartre,' she said. 'You must come and see it some time.'

'I should love to,' he replied, but at that moment he had the opportunity of introducing Jonathan to her. They were both delighted, for they knew each other well by sight as fellow worshippers in the chapel, but had never met. She promptly presented him to Emily. And then Miranda Elton came in with Pamela Fletcher whom she had met on the stairs and he had little chance to see more of Amanda.

3

When he came to throw away the letters of acceptance, he kept hers and put it in a drawer.

He was unresponsive when, as they sat up together at breakfast, the Provost congratulated him on the success of his party.

'It was going with a swing when I left,' he said.

'But I didn't make much progress with Amanda,' lamented John. 'She did say she had a picture of Paris which she would show me . . .'

'Doesn't that sound quite friendly?'

'That's the trouble. She *is* "quite friendly". To everyone. I can't understand her. She looks lovely, obviously gives a lot of time and thought to how she looks – nice natural make-up – impeccable hair-do and manicure, pretty shoes nicely polished – becoming clothes though no great variety – a good perfume discreetly used . . . And yet she seems to keep men at arms' length. Who *is* she doing it for, then?' He looked at his father abstractedly. 'Is she a lesbian, do you think?'

'Really, John . . .' for a moment he thought the Provost was shocked, but he was laughing at him '. . . if you can only think of that explanation to account for a woman who doesn't instantly respond to your attentions, you must be more conceited than I thought.'

'No.' John was still pursuing his own train of thought. 'And Emily wouldn't fit into that picture. But there *must* be someone. Or why is she doing it?'

'May she not be doing it to please herself?' suggested his

father. 'She is an artist, after all. Some women artists, I know, affect not to care how they look. But a few treat themselves as a work of applied art. In the older generation, Francesca Melzi is an example, and she, as far as I know, has always been a conscientious celibate. Or Amanda may be doing it for him. For her husband.'

John was incredulous, but the Provost, who was becoming interested, went on, 'Your mother was always marvellously turned out. I flatter myself that, while we were married, it was partly or even perhaps mainly to please me. But if I had died first, I can't think that she would have stopped minding about her appearance. She would have felt, I suspect, that she owed it to herself, and perhaps to me, to keep up the same standard.'

'Mama was a reigning beauty.'

'Well, don't you think Amanda is a beauty, even if she hasn't yet had a chance to reign?'

John could only agree.

'And talking of the family,' said the Provost, 'it is Fred and Mary's turn to provide a party at Christmas-time this year. They rang up yesterday, while you were entertaining, to ask us to spend Boxing Day with them.'

'Us?'

'Yes. Both of us. I told them that you would still be staying with me. Of course they then at once included you in the invitation.'

'The devil they did. J.E., you know that the last time Fred and I met we had a particularly awful row?'

'How should I know?'

'I thought he might have told you.' John summoned up in his mind the figure of his eldest brother, who had inherited a strong physical resemblance to their father, and the authoritarian side of his character, without much of the urbanity. 'He descended on me unannounced at the flat and started lecturing me, treating me – as he and Richard have always done – as if I were a bad little boy. I had no right, he said, to ignore the family, or to disregard you. What business of his was it? There had been some occasion which had specially incensed him: was it your 55th birthday? . . . He started calling me filthy names. I asked him to leave. He wouldn't. In the end I had to throw him out.'

'Really?' The Provost was mildly surprised. 'How did you manage to do that? He's a good deal bigger than you. Bigger than me, in fact.'

'Oh, we didn't come to blows. I daresay I would have got the worst of it if we had. I simply knew *much* worse bad language than he did.' John remembered with glum satisfaction. 'Captain Egerton had to beat a retreat. He was outgunned.'

'Of course you could outgun him. Even in something so puerile as a slanging match. Can't you see that it's one of the things which maddens him and Richard?'

'No. I don't follow.'

'Very well, I'll try to explain. It'll have to be from the parents' viewpoint, of course.' The Provost sat back in his chair and reflected for a moment. 'Son One goes through childhood and youth with no problems. Dutiful. Hardworking. Above average height. Not much below average intelligence. Has a blameless and undistinguished career. Son Two, much the same story. Not quite so tall – just six feet – and a little brighter. Son Three comes along, rather later. Quite different. Eventually almost as tall as Son Two. What are you, John? About five foot ten? I thought so. But *clever*. Can work extremely hard when he chooses, but things tend to come easily to him. One of his schoolmasters said to me, "He thinks he can learn a language or a period of history in an afternoon, and he's not all that far wrong." At the university he spends most of his time acting and swimming and still manages to get a II.i. Within two years of being set up in business he runs a smart flat in Town and drives a Porsche, while his elder brothers are still struggling up the lower rungs of the ladder in their respective trades. Now, a bit of competition between siblings is healthy, but when the disparity is as great as that, may it not put some strain on family affection?'

'You mean that Sons One and Two are *envious*?'

54

'They have some reason to be, haven't they? After all, superior age and size are the only advantages they can claim over Son Three.'

'You are being rational now, J.E. Then explain to me, please, why Fred was so offensive about my resemblance to my mother. He said, "I don't know *what* Mama would have thought of you. And why do you have to look so infernally *like* her, damn you?"' He had mimicked Fred's way of speaking with a vengeful accuracy which brought a smile to the Provost's lips. 'Why did he have to drag Mama into it? Can I help looking like her? Didn't you and she make me that way?'

'You don't realize,' said the Provost, gently, '*how* vivid the likeness it. It isn't just your appearance. Your movements, your way of talking, your expressions – everything you do and say conjures up your mother before one.'

John frowned.

'Then having me with you must be painful for you.'

'Quite the contrary. If I had allowed myself to love one my children more than the others, it would have been you, if only for that reason.' John was startled, but his father went on, 'I don't think Fred *resents* your likeness to your mother. But he must be keenly aware of it. And is baffled by your decision to opt out of her family. It was not a subtle way of expressing those feelings, but he is not a subtle person.'

'I *can't* have looked like Mama then. I was very angry.'

'You never look more like her than when you are angry.'

'But I never saw her angry.'

'Probably not. By the time you arrived on the scene she had mellowed a great deal. She was immensely happy and fulfilled in her family. When we were first married it was different. We were both young. She was headstrong. I was obstinate. We used to have dreadful tussles. Una's tantrums were fearsome. Fred must have seen them as a small boy. If we hadn't been tremendously in love, I don't know how we should have survived.'

John meditated.

'I still don't see how you can expect Son Three to get on

with Sons One and Two. If you insist on dragging him kicking and screaming into the sacred family circle there is sure to be trouble. Why do we have to go? Why can't we keep our identities? Why do you have to be "Granddad" and I "Fred's youngest brother"?'

'Because blood is thicker than water. Why else did you come to me for help? Would you have come to the Provost of St Matthew's if he had not happened to be your father?'

' "A hit – a palpable hit",' acknowledged John. 'But that was exceptional. It was a matter of life and death. I was driven back on the most primitive instincts of self-preservation.'

'The exceptional is always a possibility to be reckoned with.'

'But what would I have done otherwise?'

'Let's not think about it. I was extremely anxious about you.'

'You didn't sound anxious.'

'I should hope not. You might have become a liar and a hardened criminal for all I knew. Even if that is what you had turned out to be, though, I could not have stopped feeling concern for you. As you say, something primitive. Biological, perhaps. Because you are part of me and of your mother. One can give in to these instincts. One can also react against them. There is a happy mean. I am fond of all the family, in different degrees and in different ways. I see the artificialities and the absurdities of these gatherings. They serve to keep the relationship healthy.'

'I have yet to be convinced of that.'

'Well, let's make a start by doing a bit of homework on Fred's invitation, as we do before any other party. Who will be there? His wife Mary, to begin with. You remember her?'

Dim memories of Fred's wedding were all that John could manage. A débutante bride.

'Lady Mary Manyer, wasn't it?'

'That's right. Her mother and your mother were school-friends. She is a most amiable person. And they have three little girls, Louise, Anne and Rosie. Rosie is still quite a baby.

They were a long time starting a family. Now there is no stopping them.'

'I don't know how to talk to children.'

'Neither do I. I just talk to them as if they were grown-ups, minus the harder words. They don't seem to mind. The one thing I'm sure they hate is being talked down to. And there will be Richard and Sue, and Paul, and Jamie, who you haven't yet met – he is what I believe is technically called a "toddler". They are spending Christmas there. And there will be one of Mary's two sisters at lunch. I don't know which. One is in business, the other is a doctor.'

'It must be a big house. How does Fred finance it?'

'The house belongs to Mary's brother, so I imagine he has it on reasonable terms. And Mary is well-off in her own right. She was left a lot of money a few years ago by a spinster godmother. So Fred has given up the army, though he still likes to be addressed as "Captain", and devotes himself to the farm which is attached to the house. He breeds Gloucester Spots.'

'What are they?'

'Pigs, John. Old English pigs. Large, long and hairy. Pink with block splotches.'

'They don't sound cuddly.'

'Are any pigs cuddly? Fred has almost persuaded me that the piglets are rather endearing when they are a few weeks old. But then, the same could be said of most little mammals: a cynic might say, with the possible exception of human beings.'

John's thoughts turned to more congenial subjects. Among them was the prospect of an end-of-term coffee-party to which he had been invited by Amanda and Emily. A visit from Emily's boyfriend Martin, who was coming for the day from London, was the pretext for it.

The little sitting room was crowded. Amanda might seem aloof, but she evidently enjoyed entertaining her friends, in a quiet way, as much as Emily. The coffee was exceptionally good, and they provided delicious home-made cakes and biscuits to go with it. He saw her picture of Montmartre, and, on being pressed, she showed them a portfolio of her own work, which was quite expert. He admired her more and more. Then, when she had gone for a moment into the kitchen, he noticed Alban Miller and another of their male guests brooding over a framed photograph on a side-table. He joined them. The photograph was a head and shoulders studio portrait of a dazzlingly handsome young man. Alban looked round.

'That,' he said, 'is Simon Orson. And the card below is a certificate that he was Mentioned in Dispatches.'

The three men looked at one another. Neither of them spoke.

'Thursday this week: John's birthday,' remarked the Provost as he looked through his diary the following day.

Their eyes met. Every year on his birthday his father had sent him a letter and a large cheque. For the last few years he had ignored the letter and torn up the cheque, regarding it as a continuing attempt to patronize him. But the Provost only said,

'Dear me, Thursday is a terribly busy day. Friday . . . ? That looks just as bad. No, wait. We are interviewing for a fellowship, but we ought to have finished and made the election by six o'clock. If you wouldn't mind transferring the celebration to Friday evening, would you let me take you out to dinner?'

Relieved, John accepted.

They had dinner at the best restaurant in the city. The Provost ordered Taittinger, his favourite champagne, and drank John's health in it. He seemed in tremendous form.

'You got the candidate you wanted?' inquired John.

'No,' said his father, resignedly. 'But he was my second choice. They were both good. I would have preferred the younger candidate, who was a woman. And less experienced – that weighed with most of the fellows.'

'I thought you usually got your own way?'

'Quite often, as long as one doesn't show one's hand too

58

early in the proceedings. But it's a democratic institution. I only turn the heat on when an issue which is really important to me is in danger of going the wrong way.'

'What do you do then? Threaten to resign?'

'Oh, no. You must never do that. That is, unless you really mean it. More than one head of house has come to grief that way. I can usually dig something out of the college statutes in the Provost's favour. I know them better than anyone – even Clive. John, you haven't chosen the next course yet. We must talk about something more amusing than college politics.'

It was quite late when they returned to the Lodgings. As usual, they stopped outside the Provost's bedroom door to say goodnight before John went up to his room. By then, he had made up his mind to break the taboo which they had observed on mentioning their previous estrangement. It seemed to him that it had become unreal. He began by saying, 'Thank you for giving me such a good time, J.E.'

'I'm glad you enjoyed it,' said his father, readily. 'So did I.'

'And it was ungracious of me to refuse to accept or acknowledge the presents you have been sending me. I wish I hadn't done it.'

The Provost's eyebrows went up, and he smiled.

'My dear John,' it was the first time he had addressed his son in this way, 'that is handsome of you. I always thought there was a fifty-fifty chance that something might happen to bring us together again, if I kept the lines of communication open. The last thing I imagined was, that it would be a financial crisis. My spies in the City told me that you were doing nicely.'

'So I was, until I took on this wretched French project. But thanks to you, that will still pay off, when the new *château* is sold.'

'I hope so. For both our sakes. But we're not out of the wood yet. Good night, John.'

And now he had to complete the arrangements for their visit to France in the second week of January, to inspect progress on his building project. The Provost, who was busy almost up to Christmas with college business, left it to him to buy the tickets and book the hotels, in consultation with his secretary. Two nights first in Paris, to look up old friends and go to a concert or a theatre, then a night in Bourges, and finally a few days at the *Hôtel du Château*. It was agreed that they would telephone Henri de La Bastide and ask him and his wife to come over from Orleans, weather permitting, and have lunch with them ('It's only about a hundred miles, and he has the big Peugeot,' said John). Some of his enthusiasm for the rebuilding of the *château* and the development of the park had come back.

On Christmas Eve, the Provost was due to visit a retired fellow of the college who lived some twenty miles away. It turned out a wet evening, and John asked.

'Do you *have* to go, J.E.? It is a horrid night.'

'Yes, I must go,' said his father. 'I have promised the poor old gentleman. He is well into his eighties and his wife died earlier this year. I needn't stay long. I should be back in a couple of hours. Knock up some supper for us, John. We had a good lunch. Everyone has gone off duty now.'

He set off, and John settled down in the study with a long article which he had been wanting to read. When he had finished it, he looked at his watch and decided that his father would be on his way home. He got up to begin preparing some pasta for their dinner. Then the telephone rang. A woman's voice spoke.

'Mr Egerton?'

'Speaking,' said John.

'My name is Williams – Mrs Jessie Williams,' she said, rather breathlessly. 'I am . . .' and she described her position on the road, 'and there has been a bad accident here. Your father . . .'

John's heart missed a beat.

'He has been hurt?'

'No, no. Thank God. Neither of us. He was the driver of the car in front of me on that stretch of the road, going at a sensible speed in heavy rain, and I was following at a safe distance. Out of the blue some maniac came up very fast, overtook me and then the car in front. There was a bend just ahead and he went straight into an oncoming car. There was a terrific crash. We both pulled into the side of the road and got out to see if we could do anything. Your father had already telephoned the police. Luckily there was a patrol quite close and they were on the scene almost at once. Now there are police and ambulances everywhere. Your father kindly let me ring up my home on his car-phone to say that I would be delayed and he asked me at the same time to telephone his home to let you know what had happened. He is giving the police a statement now.'

'Thank you, Mrs Williams,' said John, mechanically. 'I am sorry you have both had such a horrible experience.'

He put down the phone, slowly.

The momentary fear that J.E. might have been a victim of the accident had unnerved him to an extent that surprised him. He tried to account for it. Fear of the consequences to himself? That was the most rational explanation. He had never thought what his position would be if anything happened to his father. It would certainly be dire. He no longer had to fear criminal proceedings, but ruin would still face him. Yet it was only now that he remembered it.

The association with the memory of his mother, whose death in a similar accident had come as a terrible shock to him? More probable . . .

Then the phone rang again. This time it was the Provost himself.

'You got my message, John? Good. I am setting off now. I waited to make sure that Mrs Williams didn't need taking home. Fortunately she has been a nurse and has seen some pretty gory casualties, but she was quite shaken. Don't wait dinner for me. I shall take my time driving home. Have something to eat.'

And he rang off.

John could not mistake the extraordinary relief and pleasure with which he had heard the familiar sound of his father's voice. He analysed the sensation and reached a conclusion that astounded him.

He said out loud, as if speaking a line in a play, 'I'm damned if I'm not getting quite *fond* of the old monster.'

He went to the window and drew the curtains back. Outside, the rain had almost stopped. Cars came and went in the street, some with windscreen wipers still working.

After what seemed a long time, he saw the Rover pass the house and turn into the garage. He ran out. The Provost did not speak until they had come in.

Then, as John helped him off with his dripping raincoat and went to hang it up to dry, he said, 'Don't bother with that. For God's sake get me a glass of whisky. I am going to sit down.'

He drank in silence. Seeing John looking at him anxiously, he forced a smile.

'You have had some supper, I hope, John?'

'No. I was too worried.'

'All's well that ends well – for us. It was a nasty business. Those unfortunate people in the oncoming car. They hadn't a chance. Almost exactly what happened to Una.'

'And the culprit?'

'He was killed too. Drunk, of course. And his passenger, poor girl. And I am lucky to be alive and intact. He only just missed hitting me. It was a close shave.'

John was silent for a few moments.

Then he said, 'Shall I get us some supper? Even if it's only a boiled egg?'

'Go ahead,' said the Provost. 'Whatever you think. We are having Christmas dinner – or rather lunch – with the Fletchers tomorrow, aren't we? No need to go to a lot of trouble now.'

By the next day, the Provost was his usual self. He gave Dr Fletcher a brief account of his visit to the retired fellow, when asked, and did not even mention what had happened on his way home. He was more concerned to congratulate his host on the publication of his book, the date of which had been announced just before Christmas.

John was beside Pamela Fletcher, who immediately began talking about his party.

'What fun it was,' she said. 'And of course my sister and I have happy recollections of that nice room at the top of the Lodgings. It was Nancy Owen's room. The Owen girls were contemporaries of ours. She used to have us in, often. Nothing so merry as yours.'

'They were a large family?' asked John, politely.

'Oh, yes, three daughters and two sons. You have brothers, I think, John? Haven't I met one: a very big man? In the army, if I remember right?'

'That exactly describes my eldest brother.'

'And isn't there another who is the most wizard dancer? There was a ball in college some years ago, it was really my coming-out dance, and the Provost introduced him to me. He was much too professional for me . . .'

'That would be Richard – yes.'

'And do you like dancing, too, John? I believe the college is due to have another ball, next year . . .'

'Yes, I do. But I don't get much practice . . .'

'And you're having a family party tomorrow, the Provost told me?'

'That's right. We are going over to my eldest brother. It will be a formidable tribal gathering.'

'It doesn't sound as if you are looking forward to it a great deal?'

'Frankly, I'm not. But my father attaches much importance to these occasions.'

'How dutiful you are . . .'

While they were driving to Fred's the next day, the Provost told him a little more about the house.

'It is really Lord Archenfield's Dower House. But Adelaide, Mary's mother, who of course *is* the Dowager Countess, couldn't enjoy running her own home: she is crippled

63

with arthritis, poor dear. Roger Archenfield and his wife have her living with them. She has a set of rooms on the ground floor and has her own telephone, on which she has unlimited time to spare, making calls to her family, not to mention her broker . . . Mary, I think, gets a little impatient. Now, these are the gates. They have to keep them closed because of the stock . . .'

They were ushered into a fine drawing room, lavishly decorated for Christmas, with a huge log fire blazing.

Fred greeted him with reserve, but civilly. It seemed as if hostilities had been suspended, at least for the moment. Mary, who was visibly expecting an addition to the family, was conventionally welcoming. Sue was friendly, Richard cautiously affable. Mary's sister Charlotte seemed pleasant.

After drinks, they went into lunch. John found himself seated between Sue, who was on Fred's right, and Louise. He soon discovered that his niece was an animated conversationalist, who had precociously mastered the art of talking and eating at the same time. The food was excellent and Fred's good claret flowed freely. Then as they reached the end of the last course, Fred leaned across Sue and began to address him loudly and aggressively.

'And what is all this about, John? Why have you got so chummy with J.E. these days? You couldn't answer his letters, you snubbed him and all of us, and here you are living with him, on the pretext that you've been overworking. You never did a stroke of work in your life. Are you pretending to be a reformed character, or what?'

Annoyed, but mindful of his undertaking to keep the peace, John answered, 'You'd better ask J.E..'

'J.E. this, J.E. that – what's come over you? Why are you playing the blue-eyed boy?' persisted Fred. 'I bet you're trying to get something out of him. You always were a little scrounger. Come on, tell us. What is it?'

It was a random taunt. But John was stung. All his smouldering dislike of Fred flared up uncontrollably.

He snapped, 'Why the bloody hell can't you mind your own business?'

They had both raised their voices and the exchange had been heard all round the table. Mary rose swiftly, and said, 'Shall we adjourn to the drawing room for coffee?'

And she swept Sue and Richard, and her sister, with the children, firmly out of the room, followed by Fred. The Provost did not go with them.

He came over to John where he was still standing and said quietly, 'I heard what Fred said. It displeased me and I shall tell him so. But why did you let him get such a rise out of you? You could have found a way to turn it into a joke. He and Mary are your hosts. You must apologize.'

John stared at him.

'I suppose I do owe Mary an apology,' he said, after a moment. 'I shouldn't have used bad language at her table, and in front of her children. Yes. All right. I will go and apologize to her.'

'And to Fred.'

'Apologize to Fred? I'm damned if I will. He started it.'

'Think again, John.'

'Why should I?'

'Because it is part of our agreement that you should be civil to your brothers. You have been publicly rude to Fred. I am giving you a chance to put that right. It is open to you to refuse. But in that case the agreement is at an end for me as well as for you. I shall pay out nothing more for you and you will leave my house with your belongings within a week. And it will be no use regretting your decision in the cold light of day tomorrow. It will be too late.'

John recoiled. His first reaction was panic. Then disbelief. 'You're joking.'

'I was never more serious in my life. If you and Fred dislike one another, I can't help it. But you needn't behave like a pair of squabbling schoolboys. You, at least, are under an obligation to act like a civilized grown-up man.'

John was appalled. Relations with his father had improved so much that he had almost ceased to think about his dependence on him still for all his finance. He had regarded their conversation the evening after his birthday as an almost total reconciliation. He half-suspected that his present threat was a bluff. But *if* he meant what he said the danger was frightening. And he had good reason to know what determination, at times even ruthlessness, lay behind the Provost's urbane exterior.

He said, uneasily, 'This is an ultimatum, then?'

'Yes. It is an ultimatum,' was the reply.

He hesitated.

'You have the whip hand, J.E. What do you want me to do?'

'Simply say, "I'm sorry" to Fred. And anything charming that comes into your head to Mary.'

And with that the Provost left to join the others.

Sobered, but still in a mood of revolt, John considered taking the risk of defying his father. If the threat proved to be real, he had at least a week's grace. He would telephone Maître Cadenet at Bourges and instruct him to sell the property as soon as possible for whatever he could get. He would contact Henri de La Bastide and ask to come and stay with them: he could probably raise the money for the journey to Orleans. Then . . . he pictured himself having to explain the forced sale to Henri. He would be shown up as an even bigger fool than the previous owner. And even if he sold quickly, which was uncertain, especially at that time of year, he had to get through more than six months before he was entitled to rejoin Mrs Howard. He might have to borrow from Henri . . . And then, severance from the college would be a serious sacrifice. There was the Provost himself, whose company he was beginning to appreciate and even enjoy . . . Jonathan, with whom he had struck up a real friendship . . . above all, the fragile but promising acquaintance with Amanda . . . For the first time he realized how much he loved her. And he might never see her again. Whereas, if he consented to utter a few words of apology to Fred, mortifying as it would be . . .

A door at the other end of the room opened, and a middle-aged woman, accompanied by a girl, both wearing neat tabard pinafores, came in. He remembered that they had waited during the earlier stages of lunch.

66

She said, 'Excuse me, sir. May we clear?'

He murmured, 'Of course', and went towards the drawing room. He had made up his mind.

The Provost had been waylaid by Richard's boys and was talking to them in a corner of the room. Fred was standing by the fireplace with Richard and Sue, and Charlotte.

Steeling himself, he went up to them and said, 'I'm sorry, Fred.'

'So you should be,' answered his brother and went on talking to his other guests.

John sought out Mary, and found her in a pantry adjoining the drawing-room, making coffee, with the two little girls. She looked up, grave, as he came in.

'Mary, I want to apologize for what I said just now. It was disgraceful of me to swear when we were at your beautiful lunch-table. I am sorry. I have said so to Fred.'

Her face cleared.

'Thank you, John. We all know what a dreadful tease Daddy can be, don't we,' and she looked down, smiling, at her daughters, who both nodded vigorously. 'Of course, we're *delighted* that you and J.E. get on so well now. Only Fred just couldn't understand how things have changed so quickly.'

'Is there really anything so mysterious about it, Mary? Can't relations between parents and children change for the better as well as for the worse?'

'That is quite true. My father and my eldest brother weren't on speaking terms for a long time. My brother was the heir, of course: it is said to be a classic case. It was horrid for the rest of us while it lasted. Then, for no apparent reason, they were quite good friends. Darling,' John became aware that Fred had come in, 'John has apologized very sweetly for what he said. I think we ought to forget it now, don't you?'

'As you wish, my dear,' said Fred, without enthusiasm.

'John,' said Mary, firmly. 'Would you be an angel and carry the coffee tray into the drawing room for me? Louise will go in front of you and show you where to put it.'

67

'You had much better take it yourself,' said Fred, gloomily. 'He's sure to drop it.' But he did not offer to take it himself. Impressed but undaunted by the size and probable weight of the silver tray, with its cargo of coffee pot, cream jug and sugar basin, cups and saucers for seven and a large bonbon dish piled high with sweets, John picked it up carefully. He saw that Mary was deliberately providing him with a public demonstration that he had been received back into her favour. Guided by Louise, he successfully crossed the room and set it down on a table by a sofa.

He said to Louise, 'What pretty cups. They're Worcester, aren't they?'

'That's right. They're Mummy's best set. They come out for special occasions. They belonged to her,' Louise paused, and said with care, '-*great*-grandmother.'

'Early Victorian, then, perhaps?'

'I would think so.'

Her mother joined them at that point. She sat down on the sofa, and motioned him to sit at the other end of it. Then, as she poured out the coffee, and Louise took each cup and saucer to its recipient, she began to talk to him.

'Do you find that you miss London? You have lived there quite a long time, I think? I know you need a rest, and Town isn't the most restful of places.'

'I must say, I do, at times. I love London, don't you?'

She laughed.

'My sisters and I had a lot of fun there in our younger days. Now, when we go, we usually have the girls with us. And that is rather hectic. Last time, for instance, we tried to show them the City.'

'The City?'

'Oh, not your sort of City. John. St Paul's, the Guildhall, the Tower – and all that. We went on the top of a bus. It's the best way to sightsee, don't you think? How do you like your coffee?'

The conversation became general. The two little girls became bored. So did he. Louise and Anne plucked at his sleeve.

'Uncle John, would you like to see our ponies? Mummy, may we show Uncle John the horses?'

He accepted with alacrity. They went out and began to walk over to the stables. On the way, he noticed a fine large swimming pool and tennis courts. He was introduced to the ponies.

'Are you going to ride them this afternoon?' he asked, stroking their noses.

'We've been out already today,' they said. 'Daddy took us to the Boxing Day Meet.' And Louise added, importantly, 'Next year I shall start eventing.'

'Eventing? What is that?' asked John.

Louise was momentarily nonplussed by such ignorance.

'Eventing is – taking part in competitions. Pony Club, you know.'

'Oh, I see. I'm sure you'll win lots of prizes.'

'Do you ride, Uncle John?'

'Well, I *can* ride,' he replied, cautiously. 'Or could. I haven't ridden for quite a long time.'

'Would you like to see Mummy and Daddy's horses?'

He agreed and much admired Fred's big hunter.

'You must try him next time you come.'

'Seventeen hands, I suppose? I should probably fall off', said John and they all laughed.

Then, as they were leaving the stables, Fred appeared. He dismissed the children with a snap of his fingers. Well-trained, they disappeared at once. He looked worried.

He began abruptly, 'J.E. has been hauling me over the coals for what I said to you at lunch. It was only a joke, you know. I didn't mean to offend him. Or you. I ought to be pleased, I *am* pleased, that you get on so well with him now. I only can't get it out of my head that you behaved so atrociously to him for such a long time. But he seems determined not to bear you a grudge. And he thinks I oughtn't to either.' He paused. 'John, shall we try to make a fresh start?'

The words were as if wrung out of him. John realized that they had been pronounced as unwillingly as his own apology.

J.E.'s authority over Fred was of a completely different kind. His slightest wish had always been law. This 'father-worship', as John had termed it, which Fred and Richard shared, had always evoked in him dislike and derision. But it gave J.E. a means of compulsion which was in practice almost as absolute as the coercion he could wield with John and which on this occasion had been probably used as unsparingly. John began to experience a certain fellow-feeling with Fred, almost to feel sorry for him.

He said, 'Yes. I should like to.'

Fred held out his hand. John took it. There was an embarrassed silence. Then John had an inspiration.

'Won't you show me your Gloucester Spots?'

Fred brightened.

'Would you really like to see them? Come on. The Land Rover's just close by. We shall need gumboots . . .'

As they drove at a leisurely pace over to the farm, Fred began to hold forth about his pigs. He talked with eloquence. The beginning of his love affair with them was evidently a story which he had told many times before, but it was none the worse for that. Having duly inspected the pigs, which he was relieved to find kept in almost clinically clean conditions, John was taken into the farm office to see the pedigrees and the rosettes and gaily coloured certificates of the prizes won at agricultural shows all over the country.

'Do you have any other animals?' asked John, having duly venerated these trophies.

'Oh yes,' replied Fred. 'We have Herefords, of course. And a few Jerseys – they are Mary's special pets. And some sheep . . .'

By the end of the afternoon, John had got to know a completely different Fred, a highly professional farmer. It was already dark when they returned. The rest of the grown-ups were having tea. The children had gone elsewhere to play. Only the smallest of the daughters, who had been brought in later, was present: she had climbed onto her grandfather's knee and gone to sleep there. J.E. had one arm round her and was managing his teacup with care.

Mary said, mildly, 'Where on earth have you two been?'

Fred looked at John.

'We've been over to the farm.'

'Good Heavens. You must be exhausted. Have some tea.' The Provost intervened.

'Please, Mary, my dear,' he said, 'remember that you are going to show me your conservatory before John and I have to think about setting off. That is, if you can tell me how to dispose of this adorable little bundle of sugar and spice and all that's nice which is immobilizing me.'

'Come, wake up, Rosie,' said Mary, picking up her daughter unceremoniously. 'We're going to look at the pretty flowers now. Sue – Richard – would you like to come too? Charlotte, be a dear and pour out tea for John and Fred . . .'

Charlotte obliged, and began to talk to them.

'I was asking your father about his plans for the vacation, now that he has given up the idea of going to South Africa. He tells me he is going to France with you, John, to see a building project which you have on hand there. Whereabouts is that?'

John still felt slightly stunned. But he began automatically to describe his plans. To his surprise they both seemed interested: Fred because they had toured that part of France some years before, Charlotte because she was concerned with house property herself. She began indeed to ask some searching questions, and then stopped herself, laughed, and apologized.

'I'm sorry – this isn't Christmas conversation at all.'

But John was roused. He recognized a kindred spirit, someone else for whom business was an ever present passion. He responded with a glowing description of the new *château* and the development of the park. He noticed that Fred was listening with attention. Perhaps he was seeing a side of his youngest brother as unfamiliar to him as his own farming interests had been to John.

Soon Charlotte was asking him whether he had someone

71

organized to handle the sales. John admitted that he had not envisaged British purchasers.

'But I think that this might be attractive to them,' she said. 'Or to those of them who have money. And there are still some. It would be a lovely part of France to retire to. And my firm does quite a lot of French and Spanish properties. We have agents in Paris, too. If you like to send me photocopies of the plans, I'll see whether we would take them on. Of course, it doesn't rest entirely with me.'

John took out his notebook.

'That is very kind indeed. How do I address them?'

She gave him the name of a well-known firm, which he had often seen advertizing in *Country Life* and such-like glossy papers.

'And I send them for the attention of Lady Charlotte Manyer?'

'Just Miss. I don't use the title in business. And have you any photographs of the place?'

'Nothing very recent.'

'Oh, I think that would be important. Some good colour photographs. We could see then how building is progressing. And even if it doesn't look much yet, you could get some pictures of the site, and of the view. And the village? Is it picturesque?'

'Not specially. Just an authentic unspoilt French village.'

'Do include some pictures of the village. And don't you think some aerial photographs of the whole park and the garden?'

John thought aerial photographs were an excellent idea. Privately he suspected that Charlotte's firm would demand too large a commission for selling the house. But the photos would be useful in any case.

'Would the local people be friendly to British residents?' she pursued.

John was perplexed.

'I haven't come into contact with many of them. The older people, I think, are pro-British. There was an active resistance group, I am told, who ran great risks to shelter some RAF men whose plane had been brought down . . .'

Then the others came back from inspecting the conservatory and the Provost indicated that it was time to leave. After a flurry of goodbyes, he took the wheel to drive home.

'You must be tired, John,' he said.

Concern instinctively stirred in John, remembering that it was only two days before that he had narrowly escaped a serious road accident.

'Sure you're all right?'

'Why shouldn't I be? I have done nothing all day.'

John was silent. He let him drive.

As they entered the deserted Lodgings and turned the lights on, he confronted him with the question that had been preoccupying him all the way.

'J.E., if I had gone on refusing to apologize to Fred, would you really have thrown me to the wolves?'

'I should have been very sorry indeed to have to do so,' said the Provost.

'But you haven't answered my question.'

'I will answer you in the words you used to Fred, minus the expletives: "Why can't you mind your own business?" Now, let's see what we can find for supper, John.'

On a fine Saturday afternoon in January they arrived at the *Hôtel du Château*. John could not wait to drive to the park to see how the building had progressed. He was relieved to see that the main house had the roof on. After walking round, and having a talk with the gardener and his son, he returned.

His father had found a telephone message waiting for them from Henri de La Bastide. It confirmed that they were all set to come over for lunch the following day.

'And I have taken upon me to book a table for four,' said J.E. 'Hotels always tend to be very full for Sunday lunch. And by the way, I have ascertained that mass is at 8 o'clock.'

John groaned.

'Surely in a Roman Catholic country and on holiday I – both of us – can be dispensed from church?'

73

'I always attend any respectable place of Christian worship available, when I am abroad,' said his father. 'And you have an additional interest in doing so here.'

'Why is that?'

'Unless rural France has changed a great deal since I was last in these parts, it can do you no harm in the eyes of the local population to be seen at mass.'

'I didn't know you were such a cynic, J.E.'

'Just a realist, John.'

They presented themselves at the village church at 8.00 a.m.

Afterwards, they spent a little time looking round the interior. When they emerged, the *curé* in his cassock was standing outside talking to some of his parishioners.

As they came out, he shook hands with them, and said, '*Bon jour, Messieurs,*' and asked them whether they were touring the district.

The Provost explained that his son was developing the site of the former *château* and had come to see how the work was getting on. There was immediate interest. The burning down of the *château* had been a great disaster for the village and the departure of the family was much regretted. They were anxious to know what was proposed. Friendly relations were established. The *curé* wished them *Bon Dimanche.*

Soon after midday Henri de La Bastide and his wife arrived from Orleans, she, as always, looking wonderfully pretty and smart. John caught himself comparing her with Amanda. Although Chantal had the advantage of expensive Paris clothes, fine jewellery and a professional hair-do, Amanda stood the comparison triumphantly.

At lunch the Provost asked them about the *château.* Henri's family had friends who lived in the neighbourhood, and he knew it well.

'Do not waste any tears on it. It was not an historic house like Meillant or Ainay-le-Vieil. It was a nineteenth-century monstrosity, *Style Henri Deux.* What would the English equivalent be, Mock Tudor, perhaps? I would have set alight to it myself if it had been mine.'

74

'Was there a house on the site before?'

'Oh, yes. I believe a plain old manor house . . .'

After lunch John drove them there, getting as close to the building as he could.

'Sorry about all this rubble – it's going to be paved, of course,' he explained, giving Chantal his arm. But when, having viewed the reception rooms, which were almost complete, they set off for the upper floors, she showed her mettle. Undeterred by exceedingly high heels and an exceedingly tight skirt, she merrily scaled half-finished staircases, evaded electrical wires sprouting from the walls and deftly stepped over coils of flex which lay in wait on the floors.

'It is delightful. Look, Henri, how elegant the detail: the banisters so prettily turned, the moulding round the ceiling so decorative . . . And, oh, what a marvellous view from this bedroom window, looking right over to the Massif Central . . .'

She asked about the kitchen . . . about the colour schemes . . .

'I like to consult prospective purchasers about the final choices,' said John. 'I find a buyer, or his wife, likes to have a say.'

'And by the way, that reminds me', said Henri. 'How are you going to sell it, if I might ask?'

'I have had a nibble from a firm in London, which has an agency in France. I am going to show them plans and photographs. But I haven't quite decided yet.'

'Let me know if I can be of any help. We are only notaries, of course, my brother and I. But we know house agents.'

John asked him about having aerial photographs taken.

'I could easily arrange that for you. I know a man who does this sort of thing and of course I can tell him exactly where to bring his helicopter. He will send you the photographs, and the bill, in England. No trouble at all.'

As they left, he congratulated John.

'It is such a pleasure to see those splendid architect's plans translated into reality. When I first mentioned the project to you, John, I feared I might be letting you in for rather a lot of expense. But I see that you knew quite well what you were doing . . . It is a lovely house, and, I am sure, one which will sell well. And the other houses, in due course.'

The Provost turned to John, when they had left.

'I can see now, John, why you fell for this project. It *is* a lovely place. And a lovely house. You just overestimated what you could do, and didn't admit it to yourself in time. I think now that you really *were* tired. You had been working, and playing, too hard. Burning the candle at both ends . . .'

The next two days they spent mostly on the site, meeting the workmen and, in the case of the second house, discussing the progress of the building.

They took a lot of photographs, both of the interior of the new house, and the other development, and of the gardens, stables and park. They took them into Bourges to be developed and printed and then chose the best to be enlarged. It was arranged with the contractors that John should come again in three weeks' time.

4

It was a couple of days after their return. St Matthew's was very quiet. Only a few specially diligent students had come back to work in preparation for the coming term and the indefatigable Mrs Macrae was typing in the college office. They were sitting reading in the Provost's study.

The bell of the front door on the college side rang. John went to answer it. It was Amanda Orson.

'Could I possibly see the Provost?' she asked. 'Something rather serious has happened to me.'

John was alarmed. Had she been burgled or, horrible thought, attacked?

He said, 'Of course. Please come in.'

Hearing voices in the hall, the Provost had already come out of the study.

As soon as she saw him, Amanda began, 'I have just heard from the MoD. It was a bolt from the blue. Apparently the remains of Simon's plane, and of the crew, have been found by pure chance by a patrol miles from anywhere in the Saudi desert. They are being transferred to Kuwait. I shall go out to Kuwait at once. The funeral is to be held there as soon as possible. Do excuse me for bothering you, but I felt I must let someone in the college know. Neither the chaplain, nor Emily, nor Professor Rogers is back yet. I haven't been able to contact my parents, because they are touring in Devon, tempted by the fine weather, and I am not sure where they are. My married sister lives in New Zealand. There are only very distant Orson cousins: Simon's parents are both dead. So I came to you.'

'You did perfectly right,' said the Provost. 'Would you like my secretary to find out for you when there are flights to Kuwait?'

'Oh,' she said, surprised. 'That would be extremely kind.'

He lifted the telephone.

'Mrs Macrae, one of the graduates, Mrs Orson, has to fly out to Kuwait unexpectedly on urgent family business. Would you please ring up and check what flights there are, if possible today?'

While they were waiting, he asked, 'You have a passport?'

'Yes,' she said, 'my father took me out to Kuwait two years ago, so all the papers are in order.'

The phone rang. There were two flights, one at 15.00 hours and one in the early evening. There were seats on both. The Provost looked at his watch.

'The earlier one would mean leaving here in an hour and a half. Would that be too much of a rush?'

'No,' she said. 'The earlier the better.'

'Then let Mrs Macrae book the flight for you. You can pick up the ticket at the airport and settle up with the college later.'

'Thank you. That would be an enormous help.' She got up. 'Now I must run to the bank and book a taxi to catch the flight, and pack – oh, dear, I have no hot-weather clothes here. Never mind. I'll have to go in what I stand up in.'

The Provost looked at his son.

'John, could you run Mrs Orson to Heathrow? I shan't be needing the car. Good. John will be outside your flat in a hour and a half. Try to let the college know when you will be coming back and we will arrange for you to be met. Now I won't keep you. I will tell the MoD. that you are coming.'

She fled.

'We must try to make sure there is someone to meet her at Kuwait airport,' said the Provost. 'I suppose there is some sort of RAF presence in the place. The ministry will know. And I will get through to the British consulate if I can. You had better have some lunch and I shall do some telephoning . . .'

John drove her to Heathrow. She was obviously disinclined to talk and he respected her silence. It was broken only by a few comments on the traffic and, nearer the airport, by the need to look out for the signposting to Terminal 3, which was unfamiliar to them both. When they arrived there, she made as if to say goodbye. He insisted on carrying her suitcase to the checkout and waiting until he was sure that her booking had been correctly made. She thanked him and went through.

The next day there was a message, taken by Mrs Macrae, giving the expected time of her return.

John went to meet her. She came on an evening flight.

For the first half of the journey she did not speak. Then, so softly that he could only just hear, she began to talk. She seemed to be thinking aloud, perhaps rehearsing in her own mind the account she would give her parents, almost as if in a trance.

'Everyone there was so kind. The consul met me at the airport and took me to a hotel. He talked with me there for a little time. Then he gave me the things which had been picked up by the patrol which found Simon. His watch. His signet ring. A tiny crucifix which he always carried. The remains of his pocketbook, with a small amount of English money and what was left of his photograph of me. And I knew then, that he really had been killed.' She was silent for a few moments, and then went on, 'A bit later the padre called on me. He told me about the arrangements for the funeral, which was the next day. I was the only one. The other relations had asked for the coffins to be flown to England. I knew Simon would not want that. Quite a lot of people came. Many of the British colony. I thought that was very touching. There was even a representative of the Kuwaiti armed forces. I spoke to him afterwards through an interpreter, with the consul beside me, and thanked him. He stood at attention and said that he was proud to do honour to the memory of a brave man who had died fighting

79

for the liberation of Kuwait. All that time I was able to be quite calm. I felt Simon's spirit close to me, helping me. But when I got back to the hotel, and was alone in my room, I sat down and cried for a long, long time. Because I knew for certain that I would never see him again on earth.' There was a long silence. Then she suddenly asked, in her normal voice, 'Where are we?'

John told her, and pointed out a signpost caught in the headlights of the car.

'Why, we're nearly there,' she said. 'It has been so good of you to fetch me.'

He took her to the block of graduate flats where she lived and carried up her case for her. When they reached her floor, she turned and thanked him. The chilly corridor light showed him her face. Tired and grief-stricken, she looked more dramatically beautiful than ever and immensely appealing.

He murmured. 'Is there anything else that I can do?'

'You have done everything possible,' she replied. 'I am most grateful. Goodnight.'

And she let herself into her flat.

The Provost was out to dinner that evening. At breakfast the following day, he asked how John had got on. He listened in silence.

'Poor woman,' he commented, simply.

'I thought of taking round some flowers, if you approve. Something like "respectful sympathy"? I don't want to sound intrusive.'

'Go ahead.'

He went out and bought a modest sheaf of white chrysanthemums, and took it round to the flat.

Emily opened the door.

'How sweet of you, John. Amanda has gone to the department. She doesn't usually accept flowers from men friends, but I'm sure she will regard this as exceptional. Come in. Excuse me a moment. I must put the flowers in water.'

He looked round. Nothing had changed, except that a

folding table, which had been moved to one side for their party, now stood in the centre of the room, piled high with Emily's books and files. She came back with the flowers in a vase, and put it beside Simon's photograph.

'And now you are here, John, may I ask you something? I am struggling with a textbook on French civil law. My French is still a bit unequal to this. I have learnt the hard way certain things, for instance, that *tuteur* and *pupille* mean 'guardian' and 'ward'. But I'm easily flummoxed. *Could* you help me with this sentence? I can't make head or tail of it.'

'If it's legal French, I probably shan't understand it either,' he said. 'But show it to me. May I read the sentence before to get the context? Ah . . .'

It was easily solved. It was not a matter of legal phraseology but a construction – admittedly a sophisticated one – to be met with in ordinary literary French. She thanked him warmly, after making sure that she had understood it.

While they were looking at the book, he had noticed a ring on her finger which he thought he had not seen before.

'What a lovely ring, Emily. Do I have to congratulate you?'

'Yes,' she said, smiling. 'Martin and I have been friends a long time. We thought the moment had come.'

They talked, but his mind was on Amanda.

'Do you know when she will be back?' he asked.

She shook her head.

'I know she has arranged to go home to her parents this weekend. John, she is determined to carry on, but she is really devastated. She believed that Simon might still come back. She has all his clothes in her room, even. Now she will have to dispose of them. She is dreading it. I can understand that, can't you? Clothes are so intimate. Like an extension of the person. I remember when my father died. It was extremely painful, going through his things, for my mother and me.'

'I'm sure you're a great support to her, Emily. Now, I must let you get on.'

He came back thoughtfully.

In the afternoon, when he returned from the library, the

Provost said, 'There's a note for you here. Dropped in by hand.'

He held it out.

'That's Amanda's writing,' exclaimed John, and he tore it open.

But he was disappointed.

'It's only to thank me for the flowers.'

'Did you expect anything else?'

'I hoped there might have been a murmur about coming to tea with her sometime, or – I don't know . . .'

'Good Heavens, give her time. You're always in such a hurry. I daresay you're used to easy conquests. This, if you're serious about it, may well be a long siege. She won't just fall into your arms. I give her high marks for having written such a nice note so promptly.'

'She will get over this, though, won't she? At least she doesn't have to live with the uncertainty any longer. I realize the funeral must have been traumatic for her. But she's intelligent. Surely she will realize that life has to go on.'

'Easier said than done. The bond between a husband and wife who love one another is terribly close. One flesh . . . Amanda was spared seeing the grim reality . . .' John remembered that he had had to identify his wife's body in the mortuary after the accident. 'But Simon's death is no longer an abstract possibility. She knows now what happened to him. And I expect she sees it very vividly in her imagination.'

A few days later the Provost received a letter from Amanda's father, thanking him for all the support the college had given her and asking what was owed for the journey to Kuwait.

John wanted to know who Amanda's father was.

'Is he an artist?'

'No, no. He's a retired RAF officer. Air Commodore Richardson. Would you like to look him up?'

'Yes, please.'

They looked at the entry together.

Born 1921, the son of a naval captain, he had married in 1960 ('Wife same surname – perhaps a relation?' commented the Provost), two daughters, an impressive record in Bomber Command, already announced by a string of decorations, a governor of his old school and of two other schools, recreations golf, gardening and writing.

There seemed to be little that threw any light on Amanda herself.

And he did not see her for several days. But she appeared with Emily in chapel on the first Sunday in term. He contrived to come out of the service at the same time as they did.

He said, 'Good evening'. To his pleasure, Amanda turned to him, while Emily, after returning his greeting, went on ahead. But she was preoccupied with something quite alien to him: the New Testament lesson which had just been read, from the twenty-second chapter of St Matthew, and wanted to talk about this.

'I am always disquieted by that passage,' she said. 'I know that the Lord was answering a trick question from people who did not believe in an afterlife and were trying to make it sound ridiculous. But when He said that in Heaven men and women do not marry and are like the angels, it surely doesn't mean that we shall not recognize each other?'

Extremely embarrassed, John could only answer, 'I simply don't know. Wouldn't it be a question to put to the chaplain?'

'Oh, *he's* no good,' she said, dismissively. 'I want to know what intelligent laymen think, those who read the Bible and think about these things.'

Fearing that he might get into yet deeper waters if he did not disillusion her, he replied, 'I'm afraid you've asked the wrong person. I don't read the Bible. I must own up. I was brought up and confirmed in the Church of England, but I'm not a practising Christian. I'm not an atheist. It's just that it doesn't mean anything to me.'

She looked bewildered.

'But you come to chapel? And regularly?'

83

'I come to please my father.'

'The Provost? But he must know what you feel about it?'

He decided to tell her as much of the truth as he dared. He found the idea of play-acting, with her, wholly unacceptable.

'May I try to explain? Strictly between ourselves?'

She nodded, looking serious.

'Until a few months ago I was on very bad terms with him. For several years I had broken off all contact, in fact. I was sick of being "J.E.'s youngest son", just an appendage to an eminent public figure. I didn't want to belong to him, to owe him anything. I wanted to live my own life. To be myself.'

'I think I can understand that,' she said. 'The Provost is a marvellous person, but he's undeniably a dominant personality . . . But go on. Something happened?'

'Yes.' He chose his words carefully. 'Last year I made a blunder in business. A terrible one. It could have been a disaster. I didn't know which way to turn. In the end I put my pride in my pocket and asked his help. He gave it to me. He didn't reproach me. He asked me to stay with him while I and my affairs recovered. That is why I feel I must do what he wants.'

She gave a little smile.

'I see. I must admit that I have had some blazing rows with *my* father. But they have never lasted for long. We have always been fond of each other.' She paused. 'I wonder *why* the Provost wants you to come to chapel, though?'

'He says the chapel is part of the life of the college. Perhaps he thinks I shall absorb some religion by a process of osmosis.'

'I'm sorry. Really not my business. Thank you for telling me this. I promise I won't trouble you with any more theological conundrums. And good luck with the osmosis . . .'

John was sitting up with his father in the study, revising his paper for Jonathan's group, when the phone rang. The

Provost answered. After a moment he said, 'Miranda Elton. It's for you.'

'For me?'

He took the telephone.

She said at once, 'John, I'm going to ask a great favour of you. You probably know that I am producing an amateur company of students called *The Mummers* this term in *The Critic* – in the second week of term, in fact. Rehearsals of course took place last term and everyone was supposed to be coming up primed, with only perhaps two or three rehearsals to do. Well, disaster has struck. A flu epidemic has broken out in some parts of the country and it is *decimating* the cast. We have understudies for the main parts, but not for all, as there are so many. The man who was going to do the Interpreter is ill. He only appears in one scene, but it is one of the funniest scenes in the play. He has to be able to rattle off a lot of French at top speed, to introduce the Italian musicians to Mr Dangle and his wife, to solicit their patronage for them.'

'I think I remember the scene. Doesn't someone say to Mr Dangle, "I thought you had been an admirable linguist," and he replies, "So I am, if they would not talk so damned fast."?'

'That's it. Deliciously English, isn't it? But John, *could* you do the Interpreter for us if you have the time? There are only three performances . . .'

'Of course, I should love to. But please tell me the dates. I'll have to look in my diary.'

She told him. The dates were clear.

By this time he was left almost completely free to make his own plans. But he took the precaution of checking with the Provost.

'You haven't booked anything for us then, J.E.?'

The Provost looked at what John had written down and smiled.

'No. Go ahead, if you would like to do it.'

Miranda was effusive.

'Oh, thank you, John. And *could* you also do the Under

Prompter in Acts II and III? There are very few lines.'

'Willingly. But I'd better have a rehearsal of the scenes in which I appear, hadn't I? And make sure that I can get into the costumes.'

'We'll arrange that. That is *marvellous*. I was really beginning to think we might have to cancel the whole show. And it's hardly more than a fortnight from now. I've had visions of having to take on Mrs Dangle myself. Or even Tilburina. But the understudy for Mrs Dangle is all right, and really quite good, and the original Tilburina is still on her feet . . . Yes, – can you come round tomorrow evening and go over it, John? Come and have some supper with me . . .'

Two days later, when he came in, the Provost greeted him with the news that Mary had had a baby boy.

'And I have sent some flowers to her in hospital by Interflora.'

'Flowers?' said John, blankly.

'Customary, I think. At least, that's what I have done in the case of the previous grandchildren. Good for the morale of the mother. And said to be good for the patient's standing in the eyes of the hospital. This time they have been sent as coming from us both, of course. You will ring up Fred? He's in his seventh heaven. He's always wanted a son.'

'If you insist. What do you want me to say?'

'Just congratulate him. And ask after Mary and the child.'

Resignedly, John reached for the telephone.

A childish voice answered with the number. John relaxed.

'Have I the pleasure of speaking to Miss Louise Egerton?'

There was a giggle at the other end.

'It's Uncle John, isn't it?'

'How did you guess?'

'I knew your voice.'

'Clever girl. I hear you've got a little brother?'

'Yes. Isn't it fun?'

'What a lucky boy he is.'

'Why?'

'Because he has three sisters to look after him.'

86

'I don't think *Rosie* will do much. I suppose later on she might be able to help find his toys for him.'

'Have you seen him yet?'

'No. Daddy's going to take Anne and me to the hospital tomorrow. Oh, here *is* Daddy.'

Fred evidently took the phone from her.

'John?'

'J.E. has just told me your good news. Congratulations.'

'Thank you. That's very decent of you. Naturally, we're delighted.'

'How is Mary? And the son?'

'Mary's all right, but a bit exhausted. She had quite a difficult time. He's a big baby.'

'He means to take after you?'

Fred guffawed. He was pleased.

'Perhaps he does.' Then, making an obvious effort, 'And how are you? What are you doing these days?'

'Helping J.E. with his investments, for one thing.'

'Does he need help?'

'He's very experienced, of course. But he says two heads are better than one. And I'm giving a paper to a group of economics graduates. And I've been roped in to take a small part in *The Critic.*'

'What's that?'

'A play.'

'I supposed so. Who is it by? Noel Coward?'

'No. Sheridan. You know, *The School for Scandal.*'

'Oh, I see. A costume play. Wasn't I dragged off by the parents to see you act in that when you were at school?'

'You may have been. We did *The School for Scandal* at school.'

'Terribly boring. People in wigs and crinolines nattering away to each other. I couldn't make out what was supposed to be going on.'

Anxious to wind up the conversation, John refrained from pointing out that 'crinoline' was the wrong word.

'There's no accounting for tastes. Well, give my love and congratulations to Mary.'

'I certainly will. Nice of you to ring up, old man. I'll say goodbye now. I'm run off my feet.'

John put the phone down.

'OK, J.E.?'

'Very much OK. A heroic performance. Have a drink . . .'

A letter arrived for John a few days later, addressed in a sprawling unformed hand which he vaguely recognized.

It read,

Dear John,

We are making arrangements for our son to be christened in a few weeks' time. My brother-in-law Roger Archenfield has agreed to be a godfather. Mary and I would be so pleased if you would be the other. We plan to call him John Manyer.

Yours,
Fred.

He pushed it over to his father.

'Look what you've let me in for, J.E.'

The Provost looked at it.

'This is indeed an olive branch,' he said, gravely.

'Do you want me to accept? I suppose it will mean attending another of these dreary family parties.'

There was a moment's silence. The Provost reflected. Fred's move had evidently taken him by surprise.

'We must be careful,' he said, finally. 'You can't refuse, unless with good reason, without making them both feel snubbed. And from the practical point of view there isn't any great difficulty. You will only have to offer the boy a suitable present and try to remember him on his birthday and at Christmas. But I wouldn't want you to go against your conscience.'

John shrugged his shoulders.

'I haven't got one. As you know. If you think it's all right, I suppose I could do it.'

'There's no immediate hurry. But it would be nice if you could bring yourself to say "yes".'

'Very well. I wouldn't wish to hurt Mary's feelings. I don't see why they couldn't have asked Richard, all the same.'

'Richard is already godfather to Louise. And they probably think that you are more affluent.'

He did not look forward to the occasion.

But for the present he was more agreeably occupied with Miranda's production of *The Critic*. In comparison with most of the cast he was an experienced actor and he enjoyed himself. Miranda described the first performance as 'a bit chaotic', but all the participants rose to the occasion. High spirits made up for any lack of polish, and the reviews were kind.

He sent Amanda and Emily tickets for the last night.

They came. And afterwards assured him that they didn't know *when* they had laughed so much.

He thought, ruefully, that he himself had never heard Amanda laugh.

And neither of them came to the celebration party afterwards. Regretfully, they said that they had too much work to do. So he did not even see her.

Eventually John received the aerial photographs from France. He was pleased with them. They did justice to the beauty and spaciousness of the park and the attractiveness of the main house. With the copies that he had had made of the architect's plans, and a selection of the photographs he and his father had taken, it made a substantial dossier. He packed it up carefully and posted it to Charlotte Manyer. She acknowledged it at once.

A couple of weeks later, she telephoned. The firm was definitely interested. Would he come to London one day and lunch with her and discuss it afterwards at the office? He accepted. A date was fixed.

Charlotte and a young man from the office gave him lunch. It was clear that no serious business was going to be transacted there. The talk was in the most general terms about the project and about France.

At their office, he was shown into a very grand room, and introduced to a Mr Melville, whom he knew to be one of the most senior people in the firm. He greeted John affably.

'Your brother, I gather, is married to Charlotte's sister? That makes you almost but not quite a brother-in-law, I think? Ha ha.'

He then went over to a large table on which were spread out the plans and photographs. He had evidently studied them with care. He seemed surprised that the project was so limited.

'You have a lot of ground there. At the moment the plans are only for a big house, a replacement for the *château*, which is almost completed, and two smaller houses, each in its own grounds, one of which is started. Wouldn't there be a case for having some holiday homes at the other end of the park?'

'I should be reluctant to do anything to spoil the main house,' said John, warily. 'After all, the sort of people who will buy it will expect some privacy. Not a shanty town in their backyard. *Vie de château*, you know. Peacocks on the lawn and all that.'

Mr Melville looked pained. Charlotte said, brightly.

'Are there really peacocks there, John?'

'Oh, yes,' he replied, turning to her with a smile. 'Three peacocks, one old and two young, and two peahens, upon whose age I should not like to pronounce.'

'But you haven't, I see, provided a swimming pool,' said Mr Melville. 'Wouldn't people like that expect one, these days?'

'I can do swimming pools,' said John. 'That can easily be added, if the purchaser wants one.'

'You believe in a step by step approach. You are a cautious man, Mr Egerton.'

'I am a poor man, Mr Melville. Only a private investor. Almost on the breadline . . .'

'It would surely be more economical to do as much of the development as possible at once, though?'

'Undoubtedly.'

John waited. He felt that there was something more in

90

the wind than selling his house for him. Then the offer came. The firm was after the whole property. And was prepared to give him a large sum for it. But he only said, 'My dear sir, that is barely what I have spent . . .'

They sparred a little longer. In the end he received a somewhat improved offer. He accepted it. Professionally he regretted not having wrung more out of them. But further exercises in brinkmanship might have been counterproductive. And secretly he was relieved and delighted to have the whole project taken off his hands.

It was agreed that he should rendezvous at the *château* with a representative of their Paris agents, and go over the work that remained to be done with him. The actual transfer of ownership, which naturally would have to take place in France, might take some time. Meanwhile, they would see John's notary in Bourges together.

The Provost was at the railway station to meet him.

'I hope you've had a satisfactory day, John?'

John told him. His father whistled.

'Do you think it's really in the bag?'

'I think so. But I shan't breathe freely until that money is in my bank account.'

His father nodded.

'We might ring up Charlotte Manyer, all the same, and thank her for her good offices?'

They rang up Charlotte at her flat that evening.

'Oh, I'm so glad you're pleased', she said. 'Don't thank me. I only got the old man interested. And when we faxed the Paris office with the details they were dead keen. I wasn't even sure that you would be willing to sell to us.'

John duly met their French representative and briefed him on the buildings. Afterwards they met the contractors. When he had left, John went back for a last look at the park. Spring was already coming and it looked particularly beautiful, as it had done the first day he saw it and decided to buy it. But his pleasure in it was blighted by the knowledge that he had been over-ambitious and over-confident.

As he drove back through the village, he passed the church, and the presbytery. On a sudden impulse, he stopped the car, and went to see whether the *curé* was at home. He was.

The priest remembered him and greeted him politely.

John told him that the park and its buildings had been bought from him by a big firm of house-property agents, who were going to develop it.

'I hope,' he said, 'that will mean the village gets some useful new residents, in due course. And you some useful parishioners, I am sorry to be severing my own connection with it. Everyone here has been most friendly, and it is a lovely place.'

'I hope you will come back, some time,' said the *curé* 'and *monsieur votre père* also. We owe it to you after all that the *château* has been rebuilt and the place been brought back to life – with employment for local craftsmen. As to the future,' he shrugged his shoulders, 'it may alter the character of the village. God knows. At all events, it was courteous of you to inform me.'

When John returned, there was a message waiting for him from his office, asking him to ring back. He did so. The secretary answered.

'Thank you for telephoning, Mr Egerton. How are you? Mrs Howard would like to see you some time soon, if you are well enough. Could we fix a date?'

They agreed a day and time for him to meet his partner.

Eventually the formalities required for the transfer of the Berry property were completed and Charlotte's firm paid up.

At the first opportunity, he had a session with his father to work out exactly what he owed him.

'And what about my keep all these months I've been living here?' he said.

'That,' said the Provost, 'was part of the agreement. The only thing I would ask is, that you should give Greenfield and the daily women a fairly handsome present when you leave.'

'I'll do that of course.'

John got out his cheque book. It seemed a long time since he had written a cheque for such a large sum.

The Provost put it away in his desk. Then, from a locked drawer, he took out a sheet of paper. It was the signed record of their agreement.

'Destroy it. No one but ourselves must ever know that it existed.'

John tore it up into small pieces and put it in the waste paper basket.

He looked thoughtfully at his father.

'J.E., I don't want to go back to London at once. May I stay with you a little longer?'

'As long as you like. I shall miss you when you have gone. But oughtn't you to begin looking for somewhere to live when you go back to work? I imagine that will take some time?'

John hesitated.

'I am not sure yet what accommodation I shall need. You see, J.E., I want to ask Amanda to marry me.'

His father only nodded.

'You couldn't do better.'

'But there are all sorts of difficulties.'

'Not financial ones, now.'

'No. But she seems to have gone into a sort of purdah this term.'

'She has her examinations next term,' the Provost reminded him. 'And she has always taken that very seriously. Her career depends on it. But look, I have an idea. Fanny Melzi is coming in two weeks' time to give a lecture here for the professor. She is coming here first for lunch with us and staying the night with us after the professor's dinner party for her. Why don't I invite a few of the art students in the college to meet her – say, for coffee after lunch – if she agrees? That ought to bring in Amanda, and give you a chance to renew acquaintance?'

'That's a splendid plan. She will come to the lecture as well, I suppose?'

'She should do.'

'Can I come too?'

'Certainly.'

'What is the lecture about?'

'About Gérard David.'

'David – the *Serment du jeu de paume* and all that? No. It can't be. He was Jacques-Louis, surely?'

'Right. Gérard David is a fifteenth-century painter. Or just into the sixteenth. He's a Flemish Primitive.'

'I'm no good on Primitives. But I suppose I shall be a little better informed when I have heard the lecture. And at least I shall have a chance to speak to Amanda without seeming to intrude.'

John set off for his meeting with Mrs Howard in a light-hearted mood. He guessed that she might be a little reproachful, but they had always got on well together.

He was greeted warmly by the secretary, and the typist, neither of whom of course had any idea of the real reason for his long absence from the office.

'You look much better, Mr Egerton. No wonder you needed a rest. You've always worked yourself so hard . . .'

Mrs Howard came out of her office. Her greeting was decidedly cool.

She said, 'And of course I must introduce you to Kitty Williams, who is helping us out. She is in your office. Kitty, this is John Egerton.'

Miss Williams got up from her desk precipitately.

'Oh, I'm so pleased to meet you. I've heard such a lot about you. I'm afraid I've taken possession of your office.'

'You're very welcome to it,' said John, smiling. 'It is noble of you to have stepped into the breach.'

When they were alone in Mrs Howard's office, the storm broke. All the things she had been unable to say last time they met, because of his father's presence, now came out. And they had been intensified over the last few months, during which she had clearly been over and over again in her mind how to express her displeasure.

94

John was taken aback at her severity. But he knew that he had caused her much anxiety as well as outraging her sense of business propriety. He was determined not to quarrel with her. He had learnt a great deal of patience, and a great deal of self-control, since their last meeting. He needed them.

She paused several times, as if to give him an opportunity to defend himself. He remained silent, waiting for her to go on.

'I have been getting some feelers about taking over the firm,' she finally said, 'from a larger organization. I think we ought to consider this. The days of small firms like this – though we are in fact doing well at present – are probably numbered. I should of course be sorry to see it lose its identity. My grandfather virtually made it, followed by my uncle. But we can't go on as if nothing had happened and this seems a way out. Both of us would be offered positions in the larger firm. It would be in separate departments. It wouldn't involve having to work together. Of course this arrangement would need your consent. I am sure though that you will see it is the best we can do in the circumstances.'

John was dismayed. He did not care as she did about the firm. It was to him just a convenient base. But it came as a shock to find that she could not contemplate working with him. He had always had a considerable liking and respect for her.

He said, earnestly. 'Betsy, I know I've given you an awful time. I know I did something disgraceful and that I'm lucky to have got off so lightly. I should have come to you for advice as soon as things began to go wrong. But I'm not a crook. I've no intention of doing such a thing again. I have in fact just sold the French property for nearly two million pounds. I have been able to repay my father, and get back on my own feet again. I will do whatever you want. I will resign the partnership, if that makes things easier for you. But we've always been good friends until this happened, haven't we? Can't you bring yourself to trust me ever again? Won't you give me another chance?'

There was a long silence. She stared at him, expressionless. Then the faintest glimmer of a smile appeared on her face.

'You *rogue*, John. You *utter* rogue,' she said. 'How can I possibly say no when you ask me like that? But *how* can I ever trust you again? What proof can you give me that you're going to be honest?'

'None,' said John, frankly. 'I can, though, prove that I am telling the truth now. Would that help?'

She said she thought it might. So he brought out the file about the French property, with the records right down to the sale of it to Charlotte's firm and the payment he had received from them.

She went through it with him exhaustively. Though it was not her kind of finance she was extremely on the spot.

At the end, she said with a sigh, 'Were it not for the means you resorted to for financing it, I would have said it was a clever coup. Well, John, you have been candid with me. Let us try to make a go of it together.'

John thought quickly of something to please her. Her protégée . . .

'Thank you, Betsy. And do you think we should keep on Kitty Williams for the present? If there is enough business to justify it?'

Mrs Howard *was* pleased.

'I should like to. The only thing is: where should we put her?'

'Surely we could share my office? We could put up a partition. It's ridiculously large.'

'We should have to get planning permission, as it's a listed building. And they would be fussy about the design and workmanship.'

John smiled.

'Leave that to me . . .'

She came to the door with him.

'You have changed, John,' she remarked.

'Older? Even perhaps a bit wiser?' he said. Then a thought struck him. 'You said the firm was thriving. But I suppose we lost a client? Major Thomas?'

96

'No,' she replied. 'I told him the story that we had agreed. That you were unwell and were about to take a year off. And he just said, "Oh, that accounts for it".'

Uncharacteristically, he was not thinking about business at all when he drove back from the office: his mind was on the hoped-for meeting with Amanda. He found the Provost finalizing the arrangements for the visit of Francesca Melzi, which was to provide it.

'She is coming down from London by an early train. Bob Rogers, the professor, will meet the train, before taking her to the room where she is going to lecture. She insists on having a full-scale rehearsal. Someone will bring her suitcase round, and Mrs Mace will unpack it and hang up her dress. Bob will bring her here when they have finished and she will lunch with you and me. A few students are coming to meet her afterwards over coffee. Including of course Amanda Orson. Then she will, I hope, have a rest. Her lecture is at 5 o'clock. She will come back here and change for dinner, which is at Bob's house.'

'Are you going to the dinner?'

'Yes, I am. I'm afraid you're not invited.'

'No earthly reason why I should be. Let me at least drive you and her to the party. And bring you back.'

'Thank you, John.'

It was half past twelve before she was driven to the Lodgings by Professor Rogers. He was apologetic.

'Sorry to be so late. Professor Melzi naturally wanted to go over everything very carefully, in a room and with a technician she didn't know. She leaves nothing to chance. A lesson to us all. Her slides are stunning. See you later, James.'

She was a big, handsome woman. Her white hair was fashionably styled; her face, which was remarkably smooth and unlined for her age, was made up discreetly but effectively. She wore a smart grey-and-white check tailormade. She spoke perfect English, with a faint trace of Italian accent, by this time slightly americanized. She greeted the Provost as an old friend should.

'And this is John,' he said.

She smiled as she shook hands.

'I haven't seen any of your boys since they were children, Jimmy. But I remember there was one who was the image of Una. I would have known you anywhere, John. You must be tired, though, of being told that you are like your mother.'

'On the contrary. I am flattered.'

'And please call me Fanny, as your father does. Or Francesca.'

'I shall call you Francesca, then. It is a lovely name.'

John liked her. She was not in the least pompous or pedantic, though she was regarded, as he knew, as one of the leading art historians. She was all friendliness, asked J.E. about the college and about his role as Provost, asked John about his work and about his plans.

'And it is so kind of you, Jimmy,' she said, 'to think of asking some of the students to meet me. I get all too few opportunities to talk to the young. I look forward to it.'

Amanda was one of the first guests to arrive. Flushed with pleasure and excitement, she looked radiant. She immediately began talking to Francesca. She was deferential but not in the least diffident. She was most enthusiastic about the painting of that period and well-informed about it. John blinked as names flashed by, some vaguely familiar like Van Eyck and Roger van der Weyden, others wholly strange to him like Dirc Bouts and Geertgen tot Sint Jans. Strange names, too, which he took to be art critics and historians: Panofsky, Kantorowicz . . . Articles in the *Gazette des Beaux Arts* and in the *Warburg Journal* were referred to . . . Amanda was innocently upstaging all her fellow guests. John was delighted by this new aspect of her and thought it great fun. He was especially pleased to see Alban Miller, who managed to intervene several times, put in his place. But Francesca, with discreet assistance from the Provost, saw to it that the conversation remained within the reach of everyone present.

98

She clearly had much experience of such situations.

John was disappointed of any talk with Amanda. He only succeeded in asking her, as she left, whether she was going to be around during the Easter vacation.

'I am going home for a week at Easter,' she replied. 'Then I shall come back. I have a terrible amount of work to do still, and I can't get the books and periodicals except here.'

And she slipped away.

He thought at least that he would see her at the lecture. But the lecture theatre was crowded and, as the Provost and he had brought the lecturer, they were ushered into reserved front seats, next to Professor Rogers. They were in fact rather too close to get the best view of the slides. But for John, to whom the whole business of showing pictures simultaneously on two screens was new, it mattered little. He could not follow the argument very well: it seemed to be mainly about the artist's development. But the pictures were fascinating and he could appreciate the mastery she showed in moving between the text of her lecture and the illustrations. He sensed, too, behind the carefully marshalled evidence, her deep commitment to the subject and, in some of the passing comments, a keen awareness of human realities.

She received a great ovation at the end, in which he was happy to join.

In the brief meeting which took place afterwards in the common room of the department, Professor Rogers said to him, 'And we owe all this to the Provost, you know. He tipped me off that Francesca Melzi was coming back to this country. So I invited her, and she accepted, before any of the other art departments knew anything about it.'

'Is there so much one-upmanship then in the art world?' asked John.

'Oh, my dear chap, the art world thinks of little else . . .'

Back at the Lodgings, the Provost appeared in due course in his dinner jacket, and was joined by Francesca Melzi, regal in ankle-length white and silver brocade. John drove them to the Rogers' house and left them there. His dinner was brought to him by Greenfield.

'A very nice lady, Mr John, sir, if I may say so. Very gracious.'

'Yes, indeed. She's an old friend of my father's. And was of my mother's.'

'So he told me, sir.'

At 22.45, the time they had agreed, he drove round to fetch them. He arrived a little early, drew up outside the house under a street lamp, and settled down to wait. After a few minutes the front door opened and Professor Rogers came down the steps.

'John Egerton? Good evening. I'm afraid we're running late. Please don't wait outside. Come in and have some coffee with us.'

He entered with his host, who introduced him to the company.

'Don't let me break up the party,' he said. 'I'm only Professor Melzi's chauffeur.'

She waved to him from the far corner of the room where she was holding court. Soon afterwards, she decided it was time to leave. John thought she must be tired. But she had clearly tremendous stamina, and was elated by the party.

'Would you like breakfast in your room, Fanny?' asked the Provost when they had returned. 'Or will you join John and me? Any time from 8.15?'

'I will join you, if I may,' she said. 'I look forward to the delights of an English breakfast.'

And she was down punctually at 8.15 the next morning, looking, as the Provost said, 'as fresh as a daisy'.

'I hope you don't have to hurry back? You said, I think, you might get the 12.15 train to London? Fine. You will have to excuse me in a few moments. I shall have to go and pacify my secretary. John will look after you. I shan't be long.'

She said how much she had enjoyed meeting the students the previous afternoon.

Although she must have been meeting a lot of people for the first time, she clearly remembered Amanda Orson.

100

'Oh, yes. An intelligent girl. And exceptionally nice-looking. She is a friend of yours?'

He found himself telling her about Amanda. He would have been hard put to it to explain why. Perhaps because she was an old friend of his mother. Perhaps because she had shown interest in Amanda. Perhaps because he guessed her to be the embodiment of benevolent feminine worldly wisdom. And she listened with the extraordinary attention which extremely busy people can sometimes give to someone else's problems.

When he paused, she asked. 'This is serious? You would like to marry her?'

'Yes. I'm quite sure that I want her for keeps.'

'But she hasn't given you an answer yet?'

'I haven't asked her yet. You see, she has been married before: her husband was an RAF man who was killed in the Gulf War, and until recently she didn't know for certain that he was dead. She was devoted to him, and had hoped against hope that he was still alive.'

'Poor girl. She must have been very young. It sounds like a *grande passion*. This loyalty has something heroic about it. You are obviously right to see it as a sensitive matter. But hasn't the moment come to speak to her?'

'I am afraid that, if I do, I may forfeit even the slight friendship with her that I have now.'

She threw up her hands in mock dismay.

'A dilemma worthy of a Petrarcan sonnet, John. No, I don't think you need fear that. On the whole, a woman will take it as a compliment that a man should propose to her, whether she accepts him or not. Of course, if she dislikes the man, the proposal may make her dislike him still more,' she spoke with a certain vehemence, as if recalling a personal experience, 'but that cannot be the case with you. She has accepted your invitation to a party and has invited you back. You have been of service to her, and shown her sympathy – I am certain, discreetly.'

'But I am not in the same league as Simon Orson. A war hero.'

'We are at peace, thank God. And unless there is some emergency, like a fire, civilians aren't put to the test. You are too modest.'

John burst out laughing.

'You are the first person who has ever said that to me.'

'But it is true – in this matter, at least. You have a lot going for you. Why should you not be the one person with whom she could contemplate starting a fresh life?'

'I wish I could think so. I fear she is obsessed with her husband's memory. At times I almost feel his disapproving ghost breathing down my neck.'

'I am sure you are mistaken, John,' she said. 'If he was a good man, as I take it he was, he is now in a place where evil emotions like jealousy have been left behind. He will be thinking only of what is best for her happiness. Do you think you have any rivals for her favour?'

'I suppose every young man of her acquaintance. But I have the impression that she has kept all of them at a polite distance like myself.'

'Then why not try your luck? She may ask you to wait for a decision: she is at an important stage of her career, I imagine. And of course she may refuse. In which case you won't thank me for my advice. Refusal must always be a blow to a man's pride.'

'I'm prepared to risk that. But how best can I set about asking her? I've thought about this. I can't see how to tackle it.'

Francesca reflected.

'I can only suggest something ordinary and conventional. Invite her to come for a drive in the country, and have tea somewhere, or a pub lunch or bar snack or whatever. If she accepts, you will at least have confirmed that she likes your company and trusts you. In the course of the excursion or at the end of it you should have an opportunity to put your case. Until then, I shouldn't try to flirt with her. Just talk about things which interest you both.'

'I see. Yes, I'll do that. As soon as she comes back . . .'

102

Then the Provost returned. And soon it was time for her to prepare to catch the London train.

On arrival at the station, he said, 'I shall say goodbye, or rather, *arrivederci*, now. I shall stay in the car, or it will be taken up. John will take your case and see you onto the train.'

John did so. And while they waited on the platform she said, 'Come and see me when you are back in London, John. Your father has my address and telephone number. And I will pray God and Our Dear Lady for your success with Amanda.'

Touched, he took her hand and raised it to his lips, as he had been taught to do in France by Henri's father with ladies deserving respect.

5

John laid his plans carefully. He would invite Amanda to
come for a Sunday afternoon on the river, weather permitting, and to have tea with him. Somewhat concerned about
his proficiency, as he had not punted since his student days,
he hired a punt several days running and practised until he
was satisfied. Finally he sampled the riverside inn a couple of
miles upstream. He then waited impatiently for her return.
Having at last seen a light in her flat, he wrote the invitation
and left it there. He added a postscript, 'Put on something
warm. It's still quite chilly on the water.'

She accepted. She came dressed in navy blue trousers and
a navy blazer, both well-worn but meticulously brushed and
pressed, over a white knitted pullover. He had never seen
her in trousers before and thought it charming. She admired
his car.

'Not the one, I think, that you drove me to the airport in?'

'No, that was my father's Rover. He kindly let me use it
while I was staying with him. I shall be going back to London
soon, so I thought it was time I got one of my own again.'

'Do you find you need a car in London?'

He explained about his interests in house property, while
driving to the boat station.

He handed her attentively into a punt and set off. It was
a fine April afternoon and the river looked quite pretty under
a hazy sun, though it was full and flowing strongly. Amanda
liked it and said she must come and paint it some time.

'Watercolours?' he asked. 'This is real watercolour
scenery, isn't it?'

They had a pleasant, rather desultory conversation about pictures, punctuated by intervals when he had to give his whole attention to the boat. Reaching their destination, he tied up by the riverbank and climbed the steps up to the inn. While they were having tea, he asked her how she had come to be interested in the Flemish Primitives.

'I had to do a year in France as part of my degree course,' she said, 'and I was allocated to a school near the Belgian frontier. I took the chance to visit Brussels. I went to the *Musée d'Art Ancien.* That was the first time I had seen a good collection of the Primitives. Afterwards I went to other Belgian galleries and to the Louvre and our own National Gallery. But Brussels was the starting point. And especially one picture there. A huge diptych by Thierry or Dirc Bouts. I thought it quite sensational and I still do.'

'Tell me about it.'

Her eyes lit up with an almost visionary enthusiasm.

'It illustrates a legend that the Emperor Otto III, misled by a false witness, who was in fact the empress, had a nobleman beheaded for a crime of which he was guiltless. The victim's widow then insisted on undergoing the ordeal by fire, which in those times was the most trusted and the most terrifying way of testing a case. She is shown before the emperor and his court, holding her husband's head cradled on her right arm and grasping in her left hand the bar of red-hot metal. By the judgement of God it has left her unscathed, vindicating her husband.'

'It sounds a gruesome subject.'

'Yes, doesn't it? But Thierry has made a marvellous picture of it. The composition and the colours are wonderful. And there is such drama. Such feeling. The wife is in full fifteenth-century court dress, very elegant, very beautiful, very pale, looking towards the emperor but not looking *at* him, as if looking into eternity. Everyone else is thunderstruck by the miracle.'

'What happened to the empress? She got off with a warning, I suppose?'

'Oh, no. She was put to death. The emperor was the type

of the just judge, who wouldn't spare his own wife when she had lied to procure the death of an innocent man. But Thierry has relegated that scene to the background, quite small.'

'Who would have wanted a picture like that? I suppose it was a commission?'

'Yes. It was ordered by the city of Louvain to show in their new town hall. In the Low Countries then they liked to have large pictures of these startling legendary cases to hang in their law-courts. Gérard David painted one for Bruges, I can't remember whether Professor Melzi mentioned it, which really *is* gruesome: a judge who had been convicted of accepting a bribe is shown being flayed alive.'

'Flayed alive? The citizens of Bruges had strong views about dealing with sleaze, then?'

'Evidently.'

John changed the subject.

'What did you have to do at the school? Teach the children English?'

'English conversation. Yes. One had to think up a topic to talk about for each class, sometimes provide pictures or tapes.'

'Did you enjoy it?'

'Not much. I don't really like teaching. But I like children, especially small children, and that helped.'

'What did they call you? Just "Madame"?'

'Oh, no. An English woman teacher is always "Miss". The school decreed that they should call me "Miss Amande".'

'"Miss Almond", in fact?'

'That's right. I didn't mind. The main thing was that they should be able to pronounce it.'

They finished tea, and returned to the river. She asked whether she might punt a little.

'I'm not very good,' she admitted. 'But I like it. And I think I'm safe. Emily taught me last autumn.'

He could hardly refuse. They changed places. She took off her jacket and threw it to him. He nursed it on his knees. It was still warm and held a faint trace of her perfume. He watched her, a little nervous, but savouring the pleasure of

106

seeing her lithe figure as she turned at each push of the pole. She was surprisingly strong. It was soon evident, though, that she was not used to so brisk a current, and it was as much as she could do to keep the boat straight.

He said, as soon as he decently could, 'There is a rather awkward stretch of river coming now. Would you like to pull into the side and let me take over?'

She accepted.

She said, apologetically, 'That comes of showing off.'

'Not at all,' he said, quickly. 'You did very well. But there's a lot of water coming down. I expect you learnt when it was much quieter. It takes a bit of getting used to.'

And, taking the pole, he brought them merrily downstream to the boat station.

'It has been a lovely afternoon,' she said. 'I *have* enjoyed it. Thank you so much.'

'May we stay here for a few moments? There is a nice view, don't you think?'

She looked at it with pleasure. There was indeed a fine prospect of the river from that point, and of the countryside beyond, and the low evening sun lit up the scene with a glow of gentle pink and grey.

He took a deep breath.

'Amanda, there is something I want to say to you. I want to ask you to marry me. I know I can never be to you what Simon was, but I do love and admire you so much. I want to look after you. Please, please say yes.'

She was speechless for a few moments. Surprise? Uncertainty? Displeasure? He held his breath. Then a wonderful smile dawned on her face.

'*Dear* John' she said. 'Yes. Yes, I will.'

He took her in his arms and kissed her. A fragment of Victorian poetry came to his mind unbidden:

> Go not, happy day,
> From the shining fields,
> Go not, happy day,
> Till the maiden yields.

107

Rosy is the West,
Rosy is the South,
Roses are her cheeks,
And a rose her mouth . . .

'Oh, don't quote *Maud,*' she said, softly. 'The lyrics are lovely, but the story has such an unhappy ending.'

'Because the hero is going to commit murder in self-defence and go out of his mind? My dear, haven't generations of self-satisfied tenors bleated "Come into the garden, Maud" to complacent drawing room audiences, without knowing or caring about what happens next?'

She laughed.

'Amanda, how *lovely.* What a delicious sound. You're *laughing!*'

'How could I help laughing? You're so unexpected, John. One moment being romantic and the next moment clever and funny as you were in *The Critic.*'

'You were laughing at *me?* Better and better. Oh, Amanda what fun we're going to have. But you mustn't get cold . . .'

As they drove back, she said, 'I must ring up my parents, They will be very excited.'

He was jolted back into practical realities.

'How will they take it? A bit of a shock? After all, they don't know me, or anything about me.'

'Oh, yes – they know quite well who you are. You see, I write or telephone to them several times a week and naturally I tell them about the people I meet. Come with me and hear what they say.'

She led the way to a call box on the landing outside her flat.

'You haven't got a telephone of your own, you and Emily?' he asked, surprised.

'This does us and the neighbouring flats very well. It would be a quite unnecessary expense to have one ourselves.'

They squeezed together into the call box. She dialled. The number was engaged.

He asked, 'May we ring up my father while we are waiting?'

The Provost answered at once.

'Marvellous news, J. E. Amanda has accepted me.'

'Congratulations, John. Ask her to come to supper with us.'

She smiled, and nodded.

'It will be a bit of a picnic, but there's plenty of food for three. I'll go and put a bottle of champagne in the fridge.'

Then Amanda tried again. This time she got through.

'It's me, Daddy.'

'Hello, Babs,' said a man's voice.

'I've got some news: John Egerton has asked me to marry him.'

'What have you said?'

'I've said yes.'

'That's the best news we could hear. He sounds a very nice chap. I know all your friends are nice. But I'm sure you've made a good choice. Bring him over just as soon as you can and we'll draft the announcement of the engagement. Your mother has gone to evening church. She'll be over the moon.'

'I'll ring her up later. We are going to have supper with John's father.'

'Goodbye then for the present. Give John my congratulations. I look forward to meeting him.'

She put down the receiver, and unlocked the door of her flat.

'Your father sounded very friendly – and decisive,' remarked John.

'He has always wanted me to marry again,' sighed Amanda. 'He took me out to Kuwait partly in the hope of convincing me that Simon couldn't still be alive. It didn't work. I knew he was probably right. Simon had last reported, returning from over Baghdad, that the plane was badly damaged and that he was over Kuwait losing height. They must have come down soon after. But Simon was a great survivor. And Daddy had friends in the Korean War who had been written off as "missing, believed killed." They had in fact been forced down and taken prisoner. It turned out that they had been sent to a prison camp in Russia. Some of them eventually got back. That story haunted me, although Daddy said he could not see how anything similar could have happened in the Gulf War.'

'Poor Amanda.'

John took her hand and kissed it. They sat for a little while in silence.

Then she said, 'I have forgotten about time. The Provost is expecting us for supper. I must change. I can't come in these things.'

'But you look sweet as you are,' protested John. 'Please don't change. I'm not going to.'

'Very well, I won't. But I must tidy up a bit, and write a note to Emily, or she will wonder where I've gone. Give me half an hour. Go ahead of me, and I'll walk round to the Lodgings.'

John found his father putting the finishing touches to the supper table.

He said, 'You will want to rush out tomorrow and buy an engagement ring, I suppose?'

John had not got as far as thinking about the ring and said so.

'Well, *I* have thought about it,' said the Provost. 'Because, if you and Amanda like the idea, I have some nice rings which were your mother's and you might wish to look at them first. You need not choose one of them. You may prefer to get something new.'

'Mama had fabulous jewellery, of course. You mean to say you've still got it?'

'Fred and Richard have had some of it. There are five rings left, I think.'

'I should love to see them and I'm sure Amanda would.'

'Good. I'll go and open the safe.'

Amanda arrived punctually. She had made some concessions to the occasion, while keeping her promise not to change. Her hair, which she had tied back with a ribbon to go on the river, was now combed out on her shoulders and she had put on white sandals instead of trainers.

110

The Provost greeted her with a smile and a fatherly kiss and sat them down to supper.

The champagne was opened, and he drank their health.

'You have hardly had time to think about the wedding?'

'As soon as possible,' said John. 'Of course, there are Amanda's examinations . . .'

'And she will need a breathing-space to make the preparations? That will get us into July?'

More immediately, Amanda wanted to see her parents and introduce John to them. Diaries were consulted.

'I don't see how I can do it before next weekend. I have lectures or classes every morning. I can't afford to miss them,' she said.

'Couldn't we go over after lunch?'

'It's a two-hour coach ride. Oh, of course, it would be much quicker with the car. We could have tea with them and still be back in quite good time. Yes? I'll telephone them this evening.'

In due course the question of the ring was raised. After some discussion, the Provost fetched the jewel-case.

Amanda murmured, 'I'm sure I shall like anything that John's mother wore.'

He thought he detected overtones of slight anxiety in her voice. Then the Provost unlocked the case and opened the lid before her. She gasped and joined her hands in a gesture of delight like a pleased child.

'Oh! Aladdin's cave!'

'My wife was fond of jewellery,' said the Provost, lifting out the tray with the rings nestling in it. 'And I loved giving her things. I bought her fresh flowers every week, when I was at home and, of course, scent and furs, but particularly jewellery, especially at Christmas, and on her birthday, and when each of the children were born, and wedding anniversaries.'

The sight of the gems, and the faded perfume which still clung to the upholstery of the box, brought back childhood memories to John. His mother, when she came to say goodnight to him when he was a small boy, especially before

111

going out to parties or entertaining guests to dinner . . . But Amanda, fascinated, was already responding to the Provost's invitation to try them on.

'There are two sapphire and diamond rings, both lovely, but quite different in style. One is almost *art nouveau*, I think?'

She turned to him for confirmation.

'Yes, that was in fact my mother's engagement ring. Then there's that diamond marquise ring: that's a nice one, but not perhaps so suitable for an engagement? Or the diamond and ruby one. Take your time. You don't have to choose one of them. You and John can go out tomorrow and see what the local jewellers have got, before you decide.'

John was happy to enjoy the spectacle of the various rings on Amanda's fourth finger. He had difficulty in making a choice among them and was glad to leave the decision to her.

In the end, she chose the more modern of the sapphire and diamond rings. John put it ceremonially on her finger and kissed her.

'An excellent choice,' said the Provost. And he showed John the valuation for insurance of the rings. This was the most highly priced.

Meanwhile she had noticed the photograph on the Provost's desk and asked about it.

'Yes,' he said, 'that's John with his two elder brothers, just before the eldest went to Sandhurst.'

'It is charming. You took it yourself?'

'No, no. My wife took it. That's why they're all smiling.'

'John looks very mischievous in it.'

'He is still. Haven't you noticed?'

When Amanda had gone, the Provost said, 'What about telephoning Fred and Richard to tell them the good news?'

John was impatient.

'Why should I?'

'Well, you telephoned *me*.'

'That's different. Fred and Richard will see it in the newspapers in a few days, when I've agreed the wording with Amanda and her people. Isn't that good enough?'

'Wouldn't it be a bit unfriendly to leave them to find the announcement in the papers – assuming that they look at that page? Why not share your happiness with them now?'

'I don't suppose they care any more about my happiness than I do about theirs. Look here, J. E.: I'm grateful for what you've done for me and I will do my best not to quarrel with Fred and Richard from now on. But I'm not acting the part any longer that you made me play. I'm my own man now. I'm the real John, not the person you forced me to be.'

'What rubbish,' said his father, briskly. 'You have been the real John all along. The real John had gone a little off the rails, temporarily. It needed a bit of engineering to get him back again, including on occasion the use of brute force, that's all.'

'You can't claim that it was the real John who apologized to Fred.'

'As much as it was the real Fred who came to make it up with you. You were both locked in a state of hostility which neither of you really wanted. If there was ever any reason for it, it no longer was operative. You weren't seeing the real person, but a stereotype, a caricature, of each other.'

'So Mr Provost played God? . . . Well, I suppose you could be right. Perhaps you knew us better than we knew ourselves. All right. But I don't see why I should ring them about Amanda.'

'Ask her. There's no need to do this very moment.'

'Why should *she* care?'

'Because any well brought up young woman would expect to be on the normal terms of civility with her in-laws. You haven't told her that you had quarrelled with your brothers?'

'Why should I? She didn't even know that I had brothers until this evening.'

'Well, I should keep your options open, and show them at least the usual minimum of consideration. If it turns out, when she has met them, that she dislikes them as much as you do, it will be time enough to snub them.'

'You make her sound very conventional.'

'But she *is* conventional – in the sense that her basic assumptions are more like mine than most of her generation.'

John shrugged his shoulders.

'You have known her longer than I have. Of course, I wouldn't cause her embarrassment for the world. I'll telephone them now. Get it over.'

He tried Richard first. He was out. Sue answered. But she had enough enthusiasm for two.

'Oh, bravo! How lovely. How romantic. You must have broken a few hearts on the way, John, but this is really *it?*'

'You flatter me, Sue. A few flutters, perhaps. No fractures, I am sure. And yes. This is it. I'm putting all my eggs in one basket, as the old song said.'

There was a gurgle of laughter at the other end.

'Oh, that was a vintage show. Fred Astaire and Ginger Rogers. A silly film, was it *Follow the fleet?* but the dancing was fabulous – and of course that jolly song . . .'

And she crooned down the telephone,

'I'm putting all my eggs in one basket,

I'm betting everything I've got on you . . .'

adding, before John could do anything but applaud, 'I hope we'll have the pleasure of meeting Amanda *very* soon. In the meantime, congratulations and best wishes from us both.'

But Fred was there in person. He at once subjected his brother to a barrage of interrogation.

'Who is she? A St Matthew's girl, you say? Is she approved of by J.E.? That's good. And her people? Father and late husband both RAF? That doesn't sound too bad. When's the wedding going to be?'

'Some time late in July. We haven't got as far as the exact date yet. Amanda's taking a postgraduate degree in art history and has exams in June.'

'She'll have to drop all *that* nonsense if she's going to get married. Especially to you. It'll be a whole time job.'

114

'It will have *not* to be a whole time job. She wants to go on with her work. She's really keen on it and has a fine career in front of her.'

'Ah, I see. A bit of a bluestocking, what?'

John was moved to mirth by this description of Amanda.

'Wait until you've seen her.'

'Nothing I'd like better. I'm full of curiosity. Hold on: I've got an idea. Why don't you bring her over to the christening? We can all meet her then.' John remembered his manners sufficiently to thank his brother for the invitation and to say that he would ask her. In fact he thought that the occasion would be deadly dull for her.

And then Fred added, 'By the way, the pool will be available for the family after the other guests have gone, for us to have a bathing party. Do you still swim?'

'Yes,' said John, patiently. 'I still swim.'

'Good. Bring your bathing things. And your fiancée hers, too, if she likes.'

John felt a little better.

He turned to his father.

'OK, J. E.?'

'Very much OK.'

'Then please allow me now to ring up people *I* want to tell. Francesca Melzi . . .'

'She was something of a fairy godmother to the proposal, was she? I'm not surprised. Go ahead.'

Francesca was effusive in her congratulations. So was Henri de La Bastide, to whom he telephoned immediately afterwards.

Not everyone was equally pleased. As he came in from the library at lunchtime the next day, he met Alban Miller.

'Congratulations,' he said, coolly. 'I met Amanda in the department just now, and saw that she was wearing an engagement ring. A fine ring, I must say. I asked her which of her suitors she had accepted. She told me it was you.'

The hostility was evident, though well under control.

'Man proposes, but woman disposes,' said John, lightly.

115

'You have the looks. I knew all along that you had an advantage there,' observed Alban. '*Homo Academicus* – University Man – doesn't tend to score high marks on that. She is a difficult girl. Marrying a great beauty isn't always a recipe for happiness, as men more highly placed than either of us have found to their cost.'

'My father risked it and achieved a remarkably happy marriage,' said John. 'I hope to follow his example.'

'The Provost? Oh, the portrait in his study – a James Gunn, I think? – is his wife, I suppose.'

'Yes. It is my mother.'

'The artist is said to have flattered his female sitters sometimes.'

'In her case, he didn't need to take that trouble.'

'I'll allow her to have been decorative, then. But Amanda is quite different. I met her first in the department, at the end of the long vacation. I was struck dumb. She looked like an old master come to life. I wanted her, from that moment. My parents disapproved. They expected me to marry someone of the same circle as themselves. Socially, of course, Amanda is nobody.'

'It depends what criteria you apply. Her father is an officer and a gentleman, much decorated for gallantry.'

'Gallantry? You think courage is a claim to social distinction? It is just obstinacy.'

'Obstinacy of a kind is no doubt a component of courage. Not the only one.'

'And she takes after him in being obstinate. She persisted in believing that Simon might still be alive. I was prepared to wait and to go on asking her. And told her so. Then at last there was confirmation of his death. I asked her again as soon as I felt it was proper to do so. She still refused. But I believed she would come round in the end.'

'Wishful thinking, I'm afraid.'

'If it hadn't been for you ... I realized when I came to that party in your rooms before Christmas that you were likely to be a serious rival. You must have wondered why I didn't return your hospitality?'

116

'I never gave it a thought.'

'It was because I feared, if you came to my house, I should not resist the temptation to poison your drink.'

John decided to treat it as a joke.

'Then I thank you for your forbearance,' he said, and turned into the Lodgings.

Word had quickly flashed from the department to the college. The Provost had told him that the domestic staff were always, mysteriously, the first with the news. And Greenfield met him with respectful congratulations.

'A very lovely young lady, sir. And, if I may say so, a very *ladylike* young lady . . .'

John hastened over to Jonathan, unwilling for him to hear of the engagement by jungle telegraph.

He was received with much excitement.

'Oh, my dear fellow, how excellent: you're made for each other. I should be envious, if I didn't have a girlfriend at home who is everything I could wish, and is going to marry me as soon as I get a job.'

John asked whether he had a photograph of her. The girlfriend had never been mentioned before. The picture was produced, rather shyly, of an enchanting *belle Créole*, as Henri would have said.

To his surprise, Amanda was enthusiastic about the invitation.

'I always like christenings. They are such happy occasions. It will be lovely. And will give me a chance to get to know some of your family.'

'Don't expect too much. They are frightfully dull.'

'I can't believe that. Tell me about them. The father of the baby is your brother . . . who is called . . . ?'

'Fred.'

'And his wife? And have they children already?'

She was not satisfied until he had taken her through Fred's family. She was evidently learning them with care, and even, he thought, with a certain zest.

'I've always wanted to be part of a large family,' she confessed. 'There's only myself and my sister and brother-in-law with two children. Simon was an only child. So many of our friends and neighbours have lots of relations.'

'You may find mine *too* numerous,' warned John. 'I only look forward to the party because we shall be going out together.'

'There is just one snag, said Amanda, suddenly thoughtful. 'You and your father will have to excuse me if I wear the pink dress. You must both be sick of it. I haven't anything else suitable. At least it will be new to everyone else.'

'What about a new dress?' he suggested. 'Isn't it a good pretext for getting one?'

'It would be. But I can't afford it at present. Let me explain. I have my widow's pension and a little money from Simon: he only started to save when we were married. As a student I had to pay for myself, because I had just enough private means to make me ineligible for a grant. My parents made it possible by letting me live at home and only accepting a nominal contribution to the housekeeping. In my last year Simon's father, who was a widower, died and left me some money: the rest went to Orson cousins. I decided to use it to come here and work under Professor Rogers if he agreed to have me, which he did. And St Matthew's took me under its wing and allowed me to have this shared flat – at a low rental but it is still a lot of money for me. So I have to be careful over luxuries like new clothes.'

John's first instinct had been to say, 'Don't be silly. We'll go out and buy a dress and of course I'll pay.'

He realized now that tact would be required.

He put his arm round her, and said, coaxingly, 'I'm not sick of the pink dress, darling. It is charming, and suits you so well. But couldn't I persuade you to let me *give* you a dress? I should like to so much. You haven't had an engagement present yet, apart from the ring, which is really a family thing.'

She hesitated for a moment. Then smiled.

'That is sweet of you, John . . .'

118

He was relieved.

'Where shall we go to choose one – that is, if I may come with you?'

'Of course. I suppose we should try Fallows?'

John turned up his nose. Fallows had been the leading drapers in the city. It had long since been taken over by a big London store with many provincial branches.

'We shouldn't get anything smart, there, surely.'

'Probably not.' She thought. 'There is a *boutique* in Cranmer Street. I've never bought anything there. They are rather expensive. But they have nice things in the window.'

'Good. That sounds promising. Can you spare the time to go now?'

They made their way to the shop. Amanda explained what she wanted. The assistant began looking out what she had in that size and range of colours. The choice was narrowed down to four. Amanda went to try them on.

She emerged from the fitting room wearing the first, which was an elegant floral silk dress. She twirled in front of the mirror, then looked inquiringly at John. He nodded.

'Quite possible.'

The next was less pleasing to them both. Then she tried on a third, which was a perfectly plain sky-blue linen sleeveless dress with a high neck, relieved only by some white stitching at the neck and armholes. It fitted her like a glove.

He nearly cried out, 'Have that one!' but he waited for her verdict.

'I should like this one, if you don't think it's too short. May I?'

He was delighted.

'That's fine. But with bare arms, hadn't you better have a jacket or scarf to wear if it's a chilly day?'

The assistant promptly produced a long white scarf, which went well with the dress.

And then she said, rather apologetically, 'Would madam allow the buyer to come and see the dress on? She is in the next room. It would give her so much pleasure. We were

119

beginning to think it would never find a customer with such a tiny waist. It was like Cinderella's glass slipper.'

'Of course,' said Amanda, amused, and she let herself be admired with good grace.

Meantime John's eye fell on the silk dress. It struck him that it would be the very thing for going out to dinner or to the theatre.

When she came out, wearing her own clothes, he said, 'What about the first dress you tried on, darling? Wouldn't you like that?'

She was disconcerted.

'Haven't we chosen the blue one?'

'Certainly. But why not have both?'

'*Both?*'

'Why not? We're sure to get a lot of invitations as soon as we announce our engagement. You'll need two. You liked it, didn't you?'

'Yes, very much. But . . .' she stopped and bit her lip.

'That settles it.' He got out his chequebook, the assistant brought him the invoice and the buyer lovingly folded up the two dresses with tissue paper and put them in a carrier bag.

Once in the street, she stopped and said, clearly upset, 'I didn't want to argue in front of the shop people. But I really can't have you being so extravagant on my behalf, John. We've spent over £200, with the dresses and the scarf.'

'So what?'

'It's a lot of money. I can't go on letting you give me such expensive presents.'

John was concerned.

'Look, darling, we're in danger of being at cross purposes, and about money, of all things. I will try to put your mind at rest. May we go back to your flat? and I will explain to you how I am placed, if you will let me.'

'Yes,' she said, soberly. 'I think that would be a good idea. And I will do the same.'

When they returned, she went at once to hang up the dresses in her bedroom. Then John asked her for a sheet of paper and they sat down together at the table. He wrote down carefully for her the name and address of his firm and the value of his partnership. There was a sharp intake of breath.

'You are very well paid, John. Of course, I'm sure you earn every penny of it . . .'

'And then there is the income from investments. I am re-organizing that at the moment, but it ought to bring in not less than . . .' he made a rough estimate. 'Knock off income tax . . .' he brought out his pocket calculator, 'that leaves us approximately *this* amount. Minus expenses, of course. We might start by taking a furnished flat, if you agree, and look about for a nice house to do up? That would cost *about,*' more figures went down on the sheet, 'and then there would be meals and so forth. But we shall be able to keep our heads above water, I think. And we'll have a joint account, naturally, and you'll be able to draw cheques on it and use the credit cards. In fact we could set it up now: Mr J.T. Egerton and Mrs A. Orson.'

Amanda, adapting herself to the new situation, began to relax. She even began to smile.

'Wouldn't that look as if we're . . . what we are no longer allowed to call "living in sin"?'

'Oh, bank managers must be used to this sort of thing by now. Lots of married women in the professions prefer to keep their own surname. It's as you like. But wouldn't it make things easier for you? You've only to come to the bank with me and provide a signature.'

'As you wish, I'm sorry to have made such a fuss, darling. It must have seemed silly to you. But I was thinking in terms of the way I have always had to budget. I will show you my accounts if you like. They will seem trivial to you, always struggling to keep within the limits of what I could afford. And although I guessed that you were better off than me, I had no idea by how much. Alban was always groaning away about his wealth. How he could give me this and that. I don't dislike him. He is a cultured man and I'm sure a good scholar, but I knew I could never love him.'

121

John looked across the room to the place where he and Alban had contemplated the photograph of her husband. It had gone. He decided to grasp the nettle.

'Could you bear to tell me about Simon, darling? How did you meet? Were you childhood friends?'

She was determinedly composed.

'No, it wasn't like that at all. An RAF friend of my father's, an older contemporary, wrote to him to say that his son was now stationed at a place close to us. Daddy had met him once. He said he was a nice young fellow and well thought of. There was to be a British Legion dance quite soon, locally. Daddy was on the committee. I had just left school. I loved parties, especially dancing. We planned to go. My parents invited him. He accepted. As soon as he came into the room I knew something extraordinary was happening. He was like something out of another world. My father introduced him to me. We just looked at each other. We couldn't speak. We were both transfixed. Then, after a long time he asked me to dance. We didn't dance with anyone else all evening, or look at anyone else, or talk to anyone else. By the end of the party we were engaged.'

'It was love at first sight?'

'That's what my parents said. They couldn't believe it to begin with. Theirs was an extremely happy marriage, but they had known each other a long time first. In fact they are second cousins. They weren't really against our marrying, though. They just thought I was too young. It was Simon's father who made a real fuss.'

'Why was that?'

'He was opposed to him marrying at such an early stage in his career. He said he was just letting himself be carried away by a pretty face. He made a dreadful scene with Simon. And then Simon stood up to him. He felt he had been long enough in his father's slipstream, as he said. Perhaps a bit like you, John, though the timing was different: he'd always been very dutiful until then.'

'So you were married quite soon afterwards?'

'Very soon. As soon as we could make the arrangements.

And the old man was so angry he threatened not to come to the wedding. But he did, in the end, because he had a great regard for Daddy and felt it would be insulting to him if he boycotted it. He never forgave Simon, though. It was a shame, because he really adored him. He never got over the shock of hearing that Simon was missing, believed killed. I at least had the consolation of expecting Simon's child.'

'A child . . . ?'

'Yes. I was pregnant by the time he was sent to the gulf. I thought, if anything happened to him I would still have the baby. But later I had a miscarriage, following a fall. It was a little boy . . .'

For once, her self-control faltered. John dried the tears tenderly.

'Don't cry, darling. I'll tell you what. Come July, we'll try for a replacement. I've never had the honour of causing a pregnancy. At least, not to my knowledge. But I'll see what I can do. You'll let me give you *that*, I hope?'

'I didn't know you were so saucy, John,' she said, but she almost smiled.

Although it had caused her some distress, he was glad to have opened up the subject of Simon.

And to her too, it had evidently come as a relief that the ice had been broken. For, when he came to the flat the following afternoon, she brought out the photographs of the wedding and began quite unselfconsciously to show them to him.

He looked with particular admiration at the picture of Amanda, a radiant bride, coming out of church on her husband's arm, under the crossed swords of the RAF guard of honour.

'But I'm rather anxious that we shouldn't have anything like a re-run of that,' said Amanda. 'For me, this is going to be something new and different. *Incipit Vita Nova*. So would you mind very much if I didn't float up to the altar in a white veil and dress?'

'My dear, I should be equally happy if you floated up to the altar in a bikini,' he assured her.

'*Please* be serious, John.'

'I'm *deadly* serious. Dressing and undressing are very serious matters to me. Tell me, love, what you would like to wear.'

'Well, I've designed most of my dresses myself, including the pink dress, so I thought I might sketch something, preferably in a pastel colour, that I could use afterwards for, say, a garden party.'

'That sounds splendid. Who would make it up for you?'

'I've usually made my clothes myself. I wouldn't have time now. My mother has a little dressmaker who could probably do it and a local milliner.'

'Ah, yes. A hat. What fun. You must have lots of ideas yourself, but shall I buy some fashion glossies for you, so that you can see what sort of things are being worn? Ascot and all that?'

'That would be lovely. And now, darling, I must tear myself away and go to the library.'

He came back later with an armful of magazines. Emily let him in.

'I have heard your news from Amanda. It is splendid. I am so glad, for you both.'

'Thank you, Emily.' And she looked so pleased and pretty that he kissed her.

She said, half jokingly, 'You mustn't do that when Martin is around. He's terribly jealous.'

'Is he? I suppose all proper men are. But he will have to resign himself to letting you at least be admired by other men.'

'If that is so, you will have to do the same with Amanda. You'll have to learn not to be jealous. And so will she . . .'

Amanda had already got to work when he came to see her the following day. She showed him two or three designs, based partly on one of the illustrations in the fashion magazines he had brought, which she had touched up with pastels. He was impressed.

'That's brilliant. You could be a fashion designer, darling. And I *do* like the hat . . . And can you spare the time to help me choose a christening present?'

She was delighted. They went together to the jewellers.

'For a boy, sir? Cuff-links, perhaps?'

'I don't expect anyone will wear them by the time he's grown up.'

'A mug, then, sir? Very traditional.'

'No practical use. Couldn't we have a silver bowl that he could use later on to put sweets or sugar in?'

'Or a cream jug?' suggested Amanda.

In the end they chose a modern silver bowl and John asked to have engraved at the base simply, 'J.M.E. from J.T.E.' and the date.

'Will you have it sent direct to the child's parents, sir? Yes? The name and address, please?'

John dictated,

'Captain Frederick and Lady Mary Egerton . . .'

Then he saw that Amanda's attention had been caught by a display of jewellery under the glass counter.

'Do you see anything you like, darling?' he asked.

She blushed.

'I was looking at that pendant with the sapphire . . .'

'Of course. How pretty. Wouldn't it go well with the ring? Let's see it.'

The pendant was brought out. She put it on in front of the mirror which stood there. She smiled at it.

'Would you like it, my dear? Let me give it you.'

'If it's not too expensive . . .' Her habits of frugality were not so easily discarded. 'But yes, I like it very much. The more so because it's not too showy: not something I could only bring out for grand parties . . .'

He paid for the silver bowl and for the pendant.

For the first time, he understood the almost sensual pleasure that his father had found in showering gifts of jewellery on his beautiful wife.

125

6

He was pleased to see that Amanda wore the blue dress for the visit to her parents, with the sapphire pendant.

They were waiting for their arrival and came out at once to greet them. She kissed them and then introduced John.

There was a distinct family resemblance. He remembered that her parents were cousins. The likeness was much more marked in her father. While her mother was still a pretty woman, she must always have been a paler, plumper and more placid Amanda. The air commodore on the other hand was tall and lean, with Amanda's fine features and blazing blue eyes, and John, as he shook hands, was conscious of those eyes appraising him shrewdly.

Her mother meanwhile was asking to see the ring.

'Oh, what a beauty . . . And what a pretty dress . . .'

In the parlour, tea was awaiting them.

'Mummy, how sweet of you: you've got out the silver teapot,' exclaimed Amanda.

'What better reason could I have? It's a great occasion.'

He father was more interested in drawing up the announcement of their engagement. He had already got out a pencil and paper.

'Are you just John, or have you another Christian name?'

'Yes, I have. John Thomas.'

'Mr J.T. Egerton and Mrs A. Orson. The engagement is announced between John Thomas Egerton, son of Sir James Egerton . . .'

'*Youngest* son of . . .' corrected John.

126

Amanda wanted to ask more about his brothers. She was cut short.

'Stick to the point, Babs. We must get this right before we gossip . . . Now, we've done John, with his agreement. What about you? "Amanda, widow of Squadron-Leader Simon Orson"? What would you like?'

There was some discussion as to whether her parents should be mentioned. They thought it would make it too long. In the end it was decided simply to put 'née Richardson' after her name.

'Good,' said Amanda's father. 'I'll get this telephoned through first thing in the morning. We take *The Telegraph*, John, and so do most of our friends. Would you like it in anything else?'

'I suppose we might put it in *The Times* as well. Shall I do that?' suggested John, thinking of the expense.

It was agreed. He took a copy. Meanwhile Amanda was impatient, wanting to talk about the wedding. She had already told her parents she did not want it to be too similar to her marriage to Simon.

Her mother said, 'But you would be married in our church here, dear?'

'No,' said Amanda, firmly.

John intervened.

'Where would you like to be married, then, darling? In London? Perhaps in the church where my parents had their wedding? I'm sure that could be arranged.'

Amanda flushed.

'I was really hoping that it might be possible to have it in the college chapel.' And, seeing him look surprised, she added, a little anxiously, 'But you're not all that fond of the chapel, I think?'

'Of course I am,' said John, recovering. 'Wasn't it there I first saw you? Yes, I'm fairly sure there have been weddings there. May I consult my father?'

They moved on to the wedding dress. Amanda brought out her designs. Her mother nodded approvingly.

'Very nice, dear. And quite simple. Mrs Phillips should

have no difficulty in making it up by July, especially as she now has a girl to help her, with a certificate in needlework.'

John caught the eye of his future father-in-law. Both men laughed.

'What's the joke?' asked Amanda, looking up from her drawings.

'I think,' said her father, suddenly grave, 'that John and I were both ignorant of the existence of a certificate in needlework.'

'Why shouldn't there be one? Just because boys don't take it?'

'Pax, Babs. Don't go into one of your feminist spins. We'll leave you and your mother to it. Shall we take a turn in the open air, John?'

John did not know a great deal about gardening, but he saw at once that the garden, though small, was cleverly planned and beautifully kept.

'Do you do all this yourself? Or have you some help?'

'I have a jobbing gardener who comes one morning a week, weather permitting. My wife gives me a hand.'

'And Amanda, when she is at home?'

The air commodore looked at him quizzically.

'Amanda likes flowers and she likes good smells. That is why I have given her scent for her birthday ever since she was a schoolgirl. She has been known to do a little job like holding a lily plant for me while I tied it up to a stake. But more often she is not available. She is washing her hair or her clothes, or she is polishing her nails or her shoes. I don't complain. She has something to show for it. She is always well groomed, isn't she? And it does me no harm. Gardening is good exercise. The only outside occupation I have except a bit of golf.'

'You have inside occupations, then?'

'Yes. Some part-time journalism.'

'You write on aeronautics? Or air warfare?'

'Mainly the latter. I enjoy it. It keeps me in touch. And it brings in a little money.'

He led the way to the garden seat charmingly placed

under the broken shade provided by a clematis trained over a trellis arch and sat down.

'Has Amanda told you about her student days?' he asked.

'No,' said John, on reflection. 'Only a few things about her year in France.'

'I can understand that. But there is some background which I think it would be useful for you to know.'

He paused.

'Amanda applied to our local university here, when she knew that she might have to earn her own living. It was a recently upgraded technical college, didn't offer a course in art, which is what she really wanted to do, but did modern languages which was her best subject at school. She was accepted. It meant a long bus journey there and back five days a week, leaving home at 7.30. When she came home, she had work to do. And she kept up her drawing lessons.'

'It must have been tough for her.'

'It was. But at least it should have been straightforward. It wasn't. During the time she had been married, she had blossomed out from being almost a child into what she now is. When she was with Simon she realized that she was beginning to be admired by other men. She didn't mind. She rather enjoyed it. He was always there, if someone on a bus or in a cinema queue got cheeky, to say "This lady's with *me*". And they could both laugh about it. Now she was a very pretty girl obviously on her own. Life isn't easy nowadays, perhaps it never has been, for a young woman who happens to be both beautiful and good. It's quite a select sisterhood. On the journey she got remarks like "Goldilocks", "Pretty legs" and "Barbie doll", and men trying to pinch her on the pretext of helping her on or off the bus. She was whistled at ... Her friends here helped her to try to look less "come hither", as they put it, dark glasses and so forth, but she really would have needed a yashmak.'

'At least she had some respite at the university?'

'Unfortunately not.'

'Ill-bred fellow students?'

'Most of the time. But her worst experience was with a

man who was supposed to be teaching her: a lecturer to whose classes she had to go in her first term.'

'What happened?' John was apprehensive.

'After the first class he talked with her a little and then asked her to come and have coffee with him. It seemed quite friendly. She accepted and went to a café with him. When they were there he began to try to hold her hand and to kiss her. He left off when she objected. She thought it was just bad manners. But a few days later he got her to come to his flat on the pretext that he would lend her a book she needed. He said at once that he wanted to have an affair with her. At first he pleaded with her, then he started trying to take liberties with her. She managed to give him a terrific slap in the face, and she's stronger than she looks, and ran for it.'

'Did he leave her alone after that?'

'Quite the contrary. He said he liked high-spirited girls and went on pestering her. He tried to give her presents. She refused them. Then he turned nasty, and threatened, if she did not do what he wanted, to report adversely on her term's work in the class, so that she would risk failing in that part of her course.'

'Shameful. Could he really have done that, though?'

'I was doubtful. But she was worried. So I thought it was time for action. When I was alone in the house, I rang up the university and got his address and telephone number. Eventually I got through to him. I gave him my name, it didn't convey anything to him, of course, and asked to see him about a student. He agreed and suggested the following afternoon. I only told Amanda that I could drive her home that day. I went to see him. I told him that I was Mrs Orson's father and that I had come to ask him to stop pursuing her, as she was still grieving for her husband and it was making her very unhappy. He laughed at me, and said that students' private lives were their own affair and no business of their parents.'

'Frankly, I would have said the same.'

'It was, in fact, what I feared Amanda herself might say.

But how could I stand by and see my daughter threatened? He said the threat was just a bit of fun. He just didn't believe that she could still care about a husband who was most probably dead. That sort of love existed only in romances, he said, and she was only putting it on to tease him. He was quite a pleasant young fellow, tall and good-looking. He obviously thought he was God's gift to women, couldn't accept that Amanda didn't want him. When I had tried everything else, I warned him that if he didn't stop tormenting her, I would contact the vice-chancellor (I happen to know him personally) and ask what steps she should take to bring a complaint of sexual harassment. And I did not think the outcome would do his career any good. And so I left him.'

'You told Amanda what you had done?'

'I had to, of course. I was pretty scared, too. She is a *proud* girl. Don't get me wrong. I'm proud of her for being proud. But it hasn't always made things easy. She's touchy about having things done for her, things being given to her. I told her about it when I was driving her back. I was prepared to get no end of a rocket. But when I had finished, she thought a bit, and said simply, "Thank you, Daddy." '

'And it was all right after that?'

'He had taken the point. Only, he was angry and took it out of her, criticized her work. Even called her a "silly bitch" for some mistake she had made, in front of the class. Then some of the young men got up and protested. And then they made it an excuse to try to get to know her better. She couldn't win . . . But she didn't have to go to his classes the following term. And after that he went away. Got promotion, I suppose.'

'It must all have been horrid for her.'

'Yes. She was alerted by it to the dangers. She began to be extremely defensive with men she was meeting for the first time. She cultivated what I would call a frosty look – you know what I mean?'

'I should do. I was at the receiving end of it the first few times I met her. I understand that better, now.'

'I think things began to thaw when she had to go to Kuwait for Simon's funeral. She was grateful to you for having driven her, and for being so attentive, without bothering her, when she felt particularly alone and vulnerable.' He paused. 'My wife and I longed for her to marry again. But above all we wanted her to make the right choice. I'm sure she has done. And I gather that you can give her everything.'

John was shocked.

'Oh, no, sir. Not racehorses. Or luxury yachts.'

'I can't see her hankering for *them*. But everything within reason. I am glad. She has had quite a hard time. She deserves some happiness.'

'I am sure,' said John,' that she has been lucky in having such support at home. And of course in having this great interest in art. I hope she gets one of these appointments. She has clearly set her heart on it.'

'Yes. That matters to her still a great deal. You are quite right.'

'And you are going to have a good laugh at my expense, J.E.' said John, as he gave his account to the Provost of his visit to Amanda's parents. 'Would you believe it? Amanda wants to have the wedding in the college chapel.'

'Why should I laugh? Oh, I see.' He smiled. ' "I don't want to know the sort of people who go to the chapel . . ." '? That's all a thing of the past. If that's what you both would like, let's arrange it. The chapel isn't licensed for marriages, so you would have to see the registrar about a civil wedding, as in France. But it is quite plain sailing. And in fact we ought to be able to save the Richardsons a little expense: the reception can be in the college hall and can be looked after by our own catering staff at almost cost price. They'll have to invite all the fellows, as a matter of courtesy, but I don't expect a huge crowd will come, especially as it will be in July. And I will consult the chaplain of course. Though probably Amanda will have someone in mind to marry you, he must be asked to take part.'

'That sounds fine. We'll negotiate about a date, then?'

132

'Straight away. By the way, who will you have as your best man? One of your London friends, I suppose?'

John thought. None of the people he had vaguely regarded as friends, men or women, had made the least attempt to keep in touch with him, once he had dropped out of their social round. He realized now that they had been acquaintances, nothing more.

'I would like to ask Jonathan . . .'

'What a good idea.'

'I wonder whether Amanda and her people would approve?'

'Strictly speaking, it is entirely a matter for you. But by all means let's ask her.'

John did so, the following day. The choice was welcome to her.

'Oh, yes. Do ask him. He is such a dear.' And then she told him that she had good news by that morning's post: she had been shortlisted for one of the posts in London. He congratulated her. But she was cautious.

'I've already had interviews for two jobs, one in Yorkshire and one in the West Country, and haven't had any luck. It was useful experience. I now have a better idea what sort of questions to expect. But the competition in London is sure to be still tougher.'

'There are two posts in London, I think you told me?'

'Yes. I may not get either, though.'

'Don't let's anticipate the worst. All the same . . . What else have you got in mind? These are both pretty high-flying jobs, aren't they? Have you put in for others, as a safety net?'

'Professor Rogers advised against doing that. He thought I would risk getting stuck in lower-grade positions for a long time.'

'I suppose there's something in that. So it's one of these two posts or nothing?'

'Oh, no. There are two other quite attractive possibilities, for which I have been shortlisted.'

'What are they?'

She went to a drawer and took out a file, taking out a sheaf of neatly typed papers.

'Here are the particulars, and copies of my applications. Have a look.'

He turned over the dossier.

'Merseyside? Scotland?. But if we're going to live in London, how would you manage?'

She frowned.

'I should have to commute, I suppose.'

'Long journeys. Think how tiring. And we should barely have weekends together. Some couples at the beginning of their marriage *have* to put up with that. Happily, we're not in that position.'

'You mean, you wouldn't *let* me take one of these posts, if I failed to get a suitable one in London?' she said, angrily.

He recognized the Amanda, though he had never met her before, who admitted to having had 'blazing rows' with her father.

At all costs, he must keep his head. He thought hard. He loved her intelligence. He loved her spirit. He even loved her ambition. There must be a way out.

He said, slowly, 'If it turns out to be the best thing for your career, and you have set your heart on it, you must take it. What I *won't* let you do is to separate us. If you go, I shall come with you. We shall go and live there.'

'But could you do that and keep on your work in London?'

'Of course not. If we go, I should have to start up afresh on my own, in a new place. I suppose it would take me at least a year to get going. One would have to get to know the local conditions and build up the personal contacts. But neither of these places is without attraction. I'm sure we could find a nice house to do up and make nice friends.'

'Wouldn't it be awkward for you to give up your partnership?'

'Frankly, it would be a damned nuisance, my dear. But a nuisance is a nuisance. For us to be parted for most of the week would be a calamity.'

She was looking strained.

'Could we really make our base so far from home?'

'I've never had a home since I've been grown up. Never wanted one. A place to live was all I needed. Now it's different. I shall have a home. It will be wherever you are.'

Suddenly, she melted. She took his hands in hers.

'How wonderful you are, John. How loyal. How loving. How unselfish. You put me to shame. Here was I, thinking still of myself and my career, as if there aren't two of us now to consider. I must talk things over with Professor Rogers. I see him at a seminar this evening. I probably ought to withdraw these other applications. Poor man, all these letters of reference he has written for me . . .'

'Don't do anything in a hurry. See what he says. But it strikes me that you needn't neglect your career if you are so unlucky as to miss both the London jobs. If we live in London, you surely can go to galleries and exhibitions, read in libraries, get to know people in the art world – we already have a useful contact in Francesca Melzi – write articles, and keep your ear to the ground for a suitable appointment later on?'

'Yes. Yes, I think you may be right.'

'Well, I leave it to you.' He got up to go. 'But whatever you do, don't start thinking that I am *unselfish*, darling, or you will be in for a big disillusionment.'

John and his father called for Amanda to take her to the christening.

'Come beside me,' said the Provost, who was in the driving seat. 'If I let John drive, in his Formula One style, we shall get there too soon.'

'What is Formula One?' asked Amanda, obediently getting into the passenger seat.

'Top grade international motor racing,' explained John, taking his place behind. 'J.E. is teasing me, as usual.'

On arrival outside the church, Fred and his brother-in-law were awaiting them. As Amanda emerged, smiling, Fred was evidently taken by surprise.

'Oh, I say . . . I mean, I'm so glad you could come.'

135

'It was so kind of you to invite me . . .'

The Provost suggested moving towards the church. There he introduced her to Sue and Richard, and Paul, who were standing there.

Fred said to him in an awed whisper, 'You've taken long enough about it, old man. But you've found a real show-stopper.'

Meanwhile as Sue and Amanda kissed, squeaks were heard from little Jamie, who had run up and was standing in front of Amanda with his arms wide open, chanting, 'Kissie, please! kissie, please!'

'Oh, look,' she said. 'Isn't he adorable?'

And she crouched down to the child's level and kissed him. He promptly threw his arms round her neck, and refused to let go. Laughing, she picked him up. Then, as he loosened his grip to make a grab at her hair, Sue was able to seize him and take him over.

'Oh, what manners. Naughty boy.'

'He's going to be a breaker of hearts,' commented Amanda.

'In the meantime he's a breaker of everything else in sight,' said his father. 'A dear little horror, in fact.'

Jamie, undefeated, began to protest loudly at being separated from the 'pretty lady'.

Then, spotting his grandfather, he changed his tune, and began bawling, 'Jay-ee! Jay-ee! – '

By that time, Mary and the baby had arrived, driven by her sister Charlotte, and it was time to go into church.

John had to join them and Fred and his co-godfather Roger Archenfield, at the font, while the Provost offered Amanda his arm and escorted her to the front pew.

The service passed off without incident.

Fred made a point of coming out of church at the same time as Amanda and John.

She turned to him, and said, 'What nice hymns we had. "Stand up, stand up, for Jesus" was such a clever choice for a christening.'

Fred beamed.

'It is my favourite hymn.'

'It is a splendid hymn. Especially to that rousing martial tune – I think it's called "Morning Light"?'

'I didn't know what it was called. But it's a good name for a cheerful hymn. Now, you must meet the parson . . .'

To him, she made some innocuous remark about the date of the church.

'You are quite right, Mrs Orson,' he replied, indulgently, 'It *is* fourteenth-century. Such a pity we have that *dreadful* Victorian east window.'

John trembled for him. He had noticed the stained glass window in the chancel, which he took to be Pre-Raphaelite, and he knew that Amanda particularly liked that style. But she was evidently practised in the art of dealing with philistines without being impolite.

'Oh, I don't think you need feel that you have to apologize for it, Vicar,' she said. 'It isn't every day that one walks into a country church and meets Sir Edward Burne-Jones. It *is* Burne-Jones, isn't it?'

'You must ask Lord Archenfield,' he said, lamely. 'His family I believe gave the window . . .'

She thanked him sweetly for the information.

They they adjourned to Fred's house, or rather to his garden, for it was a fine summer afternoon and tea was served out of doors.

Amanda was immediately swept off to be introduced to Mary and the baby.

The Provost, seeing John momentarily on his own, said, 'I would like you to meet Adelaide, Mary's mother. You probably haven't seen each other since Fred's wedding. She knows about your engagement and would like to congratulate you. She was one of your mother's bridesmaids, you know.'

John had noticed his father talking to an old lady in a wheelchair. Unwillingly he agreed. Totally unused to dealing with aged or disabled people, he found the dowager countess forbidding, though it seemed she was trying to be pleasant.

137

A moment later her son Roger came up with Amanda.

'Oh, well met, John. May I have the pleasure of introducing your fiancée to my mother? . . . Mama, she was asking me about the stained glass window in the church. You know more about that than I do.'

He firmly brought up a garden chair for Amanda, who, to John's dismay, sat down readily beside the old lady and began to talk to her. Plainly she had not only social poise but a highly developed social conscience. He was obliged to content himself with helping to provide them both with tea and cakes, and let himself be taken off to be introduced to the present Lady Archenfield. He was a little consoled to find that she was French, and happy, though she spoke excellent English, to converse with him in her native language.

Eventually the friends and neighbours who had been invited began to leave and finally the Archenfields departed too. Mary and the child had disappeared indoors. Fred then announced that the swimming pool awaited them.

John followed his directions to cloakrooms which gave access to the garden by a side door. Benefiting from almost daily practice, he changed more swiftly than any of the others, and came out wearing his bathing shorts and carrying his towel to find Amanda and his father sitting in deckchairs by the pool under an awning. He sat down at her feet with a sigh of happiness. After a moment he felt her hand on his bare shoulder. It was the briefest, the most discreet of caresses, but it was the first of its kind. He turned and smiled up at her.

'Aren't you going in, darling?' she asked.

'I think I ought perhaps to wait for the others,' he said.

But the Provost reassured him.

'I'm sure you needn't. Give us an exhibition, John. The pool will soon be too full of people to move.'

Delighted at being invited to show off in front of Amanda, he got up and ran to the diving board, making an elegant entry into the water. As he surfaced, he heard cries of 'Bravo!' and saw that Paul and Louise had just arrived.

138

'Oh, I wish I could dive like that, with a somersault!' cried Paul.

'You will,' John assured him. 'It's only a matter of practice.'

Louise had already got in. She looked fetching in her swimsuit. John offered to take her to the deep end. She shook her head.

'I don't go out of my depth yet.'

'But I'll give you a ride. You'll be quite safe. I won't let you drown.'

'A ride? But how? Piggyback?'

'No, the other way up, as we do in life-saving. I'll hold you.'

'But can you swim without using your arms?'

'Oh, yes. It's quite easy just with your legs.'

Louise let herself be persuaded. Her fears soon subsided.
'Oooh, what fun . . .'

'Don't wriggle or we may capsize,' warned John.

He looked over his shoulder to see how close they were to the end and brought the little girl safely to the steps.

They sat down together by the side of the pool. She looked at him meditatively.

'Uncle John.'

'Yes?'

'You and Amanda are engaged?'

'Certainly.'

'That means: you are going to be married?'

'Quite right.'

'So there will be a wedding?'

'Right again.'

'Shall we be allowed to come?'

'Of course.'

'Shall Anne and I be bridesmaids?'

'Bridesmaids?' John was taken by surprise. 'I don't know what Amanda has in mind, Louise – yet. I know she wants a very simple wedding. You see, her first husband isn't alive any more, but she loved him a great deal and she's still sad about him. So she's not going to wear a white dress and veil and all that.'

'Oh.' Louise looked thoughtful. 'What's she going to wear, then? An ordinary frock?'

'A pretty frock. The sort of thing you'd go to a garden party in.'

'But she'd carry a bouquet?'

'I expect so.'

'Then she'll need someone to take the bouquet from her before she gets the ring.'

John smiled.

'You know more about it than I do, Louise.'

'But will you ask her, Uncle John? Whether we can be bridesmaids?'

The question was so wistful that he could not refuse.

By that time Fred had arrived with her younger sister, Anne. In bathing array, and no longer camouflaged by a well-cut suit, he was still a fine figure of a man but decidedly stout, as John remarked with malice on returning briefly to the spectators.

'Mary feeds him too well,' responded his father, dryly.

Richard, who arrived next with Sue and Jamie, was in distinctly better shape. Regular ballroom dancing, John concluded, helped to keep in training. Sue also seemed svelte, though he could not see much more than a pair of shapely legs: she was concentrating on helping Jamie, who was still learning to swim, and did not discard a loose beach shirt which she was wearing over her swimsuit.

Richard left Jamie to her, and, looking up, called out, 'Come on, John! Race you to the other end and back?'

'Done!' said John, at once.

The brothers set off in style. John was the better swimmer, but Richard was the more powerful man. It was a dead heat.

Soon, as J.E. had predicted, the pool was too crowded for real sport and it was echoing to the squeals of happy children.

John was in no hurry to leave. But, unlike Richard and Sue, who were spending the night there, he had to think of the drive home. Amanda might be tired. The Provost looked at his watch.

140

'Perhaps you might slip away in a few minutes and change? We mustn't be too late setting off . . .'

The necessary goodbyes having been said, they went to the car. This time John was allowed to drive. On their return, he put down his father at the Lodgings, and took Amanda round to her flat.

'I hope you're not fatigued, darling?' he enquired.

'Oh, no,' she answered, surprised. 'It has been a marvellous day. Yours is such a *lovely* family, John. They all made me so welcome. Your godson is the *sweetest* baby. And you were splendid. You were so charming to everyone, so sweet with the children, you swam so beautifully, you looked so handsome . . .'

'Really, my dear, you'll turn my head. It was you who stole the show. I'm only sorry that you were stuck for such a long time with that dreadful crone.'

'Dreadful crone? You don't mean Mary's mother?'

'Of course I do. Isn't she an absolute death's head? A face like old boots, bloodshot eyes, scraggy neck, horrible deformed hands . . .'

'Stop, stop, John. *I* should be a crone if I was that age and suffered from that awful arthritis.'

'Age? A contemporary of my mother's? She can't be even as old as J.E.'

'Constant pain can make people prematurely aged.'

'Can't she take drugs for it?'

'There are painkillers, of course. But they tend to put the mind into a sort of daze. She doesn't want to resort to them too much. She is very alert mentally.'

'Well, she's a horrid sight, anyway. She might at least refrain from appearing in public.'

'Why should she? The poor dear has little enough fun, though she tells me she is well looked after at home. Today it was giving her pleasure to meet her extended family. She was delighted to see you. You reminded her of your mother.'

'I still don't see why Roger doesn't put her into a decent nursing home.'

'How hard-hearted you are, John.'

'Hard-hearted?'

She corrected herself.

'I'm sorry. I shouldn't have said that. I'm sure you're not. Perhaps it is that you haven't got over the stage of physical repulsion.'

'Physical repulsion. Yes, that's it. Don't you feel it too?'

With some effort, she recollected being taken by her mother to visit sick, blind and crippled people, some of whom had rather frightened her, when she was small.

'I remember feeling it as a child. I don't think about it much now. I try to concentrate on communicating with the person. But John, Adelaide is *sweet.* I had *such* an interesting talk with her. She really knows a lot about art, especially Italian art. She and her husband travelled a great deal in Italy. She has the most wonderfully precise recollections of what she saw. She told me that she kept detailed diaries, and she constantly rereads them, and looks up books which have pictures of the art galleries they visited. It is a great solace to her. I even managed to talk some Italian with her. She said hers was rusty but it was better than mine: I haven't been in Italy much, alas.'

'And you asked her about the stained-glass window?'

'Oh, of course. I was going to tell you. She had heard about it from her in-laws. The family had planned the window to commemorate the queen's Jubilee in 1887. There was only plain glass in the church before that. She remembers being shown the designs which the artist submitted.'

'Would the Archenfields still have them?'

'She thinks it's possible. The family have a tendency never to throw things away, she says. She is going to look.'

'But that would be of great interest to you, wouldn't it, darling? There might even be correspondence?'

'I thought the same thing. And she wants us to come over and see their pictures, too. They have a Reynolds portrait, and "two or three" Gainsboroughs, did you know?, oh, and a Poussin, quite an important work if it's the one I think it is from her description.'

'Well, you seem to got quite a lot out of the hag – sorry,

142

darling, I mean the dear old lady. Perhaps it wasn't time wasted sitting up with her. We'll see whether anything comes of it.'

The next day, John came in to the Lodgings after a walk a little after midday. His father was not yet back from church. He found Greenfield taking a telephone call in the study.

'Very good, my lord. I'll give him the message. Just a minute, sir, I think he's just come in . . . Mr John, the Earl of Archenfield to speak to you.'

John took the telephone from him.

'Roger, hello?'

'Hello, John. I wanted to let you know that we have found the designs for the stained-glass window and some letters about ordering and paying for it. My mother was dead set on looking for them. Churchgoing was abandoned. I've spent most of the morning helping her to go through the drawers in my grandfather's desk in the library. I have only used it from time to time to look up old records of farms and suchlike. In the end we came on the things in a drawer full of stuff about the 1887 Jubilee. My mother is quite delighted. She took a great fancy to Amanda, well, who wouldn't? and insisted that I should ring you up straight away.'

'How very good of you to have been to so much trouble. I know Amanda will be thrilled.'

'The next thing is for her to see them. Unfortunately I have to be in London all this coming week. But my mother and Geneviève will be here and would love to show her, or both of you, the papers we've found and, of course, anything else in the house that you would like to see. Any afternoon Monday to Thursday inclusive. Geneviève has a tea party somewhere on Friday and on Saturday the house is open to the public in aid of the Red Cross.'

'That is most kind. May I consult with Amanda and ring you back?'

'Of course. I think J.E. has our number . . . Curious, isn't it? I have looked at that window more or less every Sunday

143

since I was a child and have never thought about how it came to be there. It was just part of the landscape.'

On the day agreed, they set off, stopping first at the church, where Amanda wanted to sketch the window. Arriving there, she sought out a good position and sat down with her pad and pencil. John watched intently as the drawing took shape: first the outline of the tracery, then the allegorical figures which were the main feature of the iconography, then a record of the surrounding decoration and, finally, the armorial bearings and inscriptions at the base. Then he remembered that he had offered to take some colour photographs, if the light were favourable, and went off to study the conditions. He took several pictures from various points. Returning to Amanda, he waited until she was satisfied with what she had drawn. It was then time to go to their appointment with the Archenfields.

Geneviève was there to greet them and brought them into the house. They saw over it, under her guidance. Then she called her mother-in-law.

Countess Adelaide came out from her room, walking painfully on two sticks, a watchful young carer at her elbow who retreated after being introduced and seeing her patient into a chair. She talked to them affectionately and then suggested that Geneviève should take Amanda into the library and let her see the papers which had been found for her. Left alone with her, John made a manful effort to converse.

Remembering something J.E. had said, he began, 'I believe you were at school with my mother? Is it indiscreet to ask what she was like then?'

'*Very* indiscreet,' came the answer. 'But why shouldn't I tell you? Una was the prettiest of us. She was also the naughtiest.'

'How naughty?' he inquired, interested.

'Well ... I should explain that it was a convent school, run by Anglican nuns. We were all in great awe of them, especially of the mother superior, all except Una. She treated them light-heartedly. I don't mean that she was irre-

144

ligious, but she was disrespectful, mimicked them to perfection, didn't mind getting into scrapes.'

'What sort of scrapes?'

'Oh, mostly just disregarding minor rules. The craziest escapade wasn't a scrape at all because the school never found out that it had happened. Going to that dance ... But you must have heard about that from your father?'

'Not a word.'

'Well,' Adelaide settled down to her story with obvious relish, 'in our last year he invited her to a Spring Ball at St Matthew's. He was already an undergraduate, of course. The nuns sometimes allowed senior girls to go to dances and made proper arrangements for them to be let into the school when they returned, providing it was not after, I think, 2 o'clock. So Una went to the mother superior to ask permission. It was refused. She pretended to be disappointed but to accept the decision. She went straight back and wrote to James, explaining, and telling him where to pick her up some little distance from the school.'

'And she went to the ball?'

'Yes, she did. She persuaded one of our friends who was a prefect, who had a room of her own on the ground floor, with shutters which she locked at night, to let her in when she came back. There was a park wall round the convent grounds, which must have been at least eight feet high: none of us thought she could possibly make it, even though she was a star performer in the gym. When the evening came she got ready, tucked up her dance dress, a long one, of course, round her waist under a coat, carried her party shoes in a bag, and walked quietly out of the gate.'

'And she got back all right?'

'Oh, yes. We asked her how she managed the wall. She said, "I took off my dress and made a bundle of it and threw it over the wall, and my shoes, and Jimmy lifted me up so that I stood on his shoulders and held me. When I was safely over, he threw me my coat and my outdoor shoes." Her only anxiety was afterwards to make the girl hear who had promised to let her in, without waking other people.'

145

'She wasn't caught, then? Or hurt?'

'She got her hands grazed and her knees bruised. But she said it had been a marvellous evening. She was up at seven a usual when the bell rang and appeared at mass as if butter wouldn't melt in her mouth. She *was* a madcap in those days.' Adelaide shook with laughter at the recollection. 'Oh, she was always lucky. Until that dreadful accident . . . Don't let us think about it. She had a happy life until then. They were married soon after James took his degree and we were married the following year.' She paused, and added, thoughtfully, 'Some of James's wilder contemporaries no doubt had helped half-naked young women to climb in over college or convent walls at night. I should be surprised if *he* had. But he would have done anything for Una. He had for some time been one of her most fancied admirers. Her only serious reservation was that she thought he was a rather *staid* young man. After the way he had risen to the occasion that night, she decided that he was the man for her.'

Then Amanda and Geneviève returned, carrying a bundle of papers.

'It's marvellous,' declared Amanda, bubbling with excitement. 'There are alternative designs for the window and letters about it and receipts – and all sorts of things. And Lord Archenfield has been so kind as to type and sign a statement authorizing me to borrow them, to have them photographed and to publish something about them in due course, with the usual acknowledgements.'

'You can borrow them, darling? Actually take them home to study?' exclaimed John. 'How splendid.' And he turned to Adelaide. 'We owe all this to you, don't we? How good of you. It must have been a terrific job to look for them. When you weren't even sure that they were there? And how generous of Roger . . .'

On the way home, Amanda talked non-stop about the papers she had been lent about the inception and execution of the window.

When she drew breath, she said, 'And I was *so* pleased

146

that you seemed to be getting on better with Adelaide. I heard both of you laughing when I came out of the library.'

'Oh, yes,' he replied, 'I took your advice and concentrated on communicating with the person. It worked well.'

He decided to wait until he knew her better before telling her the subject of their laughter. He had himself heard Adelaide's story about his parents with an admiring amusement. He was not sure that Amanda's reaction would be the same. He suspected that she had a rather prim side to her. But when he came back to the Lodgings, he could not resist the temptation to quiz his father about it.

'She told you that, did she?' said the Provost. 'She liked fun too, in her own way. She was a most tremendous flirt, much more so than Una. But she wasn't so daring. Una was quite fearless. She thought the whole thing was a huge joke, the perfect climax to a jolly evening. She had warned me that there was a wall to get over. I was aghast when I saw how high it was. She said it was quite safe, that she had prospected it from the other side and knew that there was soft open ground to fall onto at that point. I was terrified that I might drop her (it gave me a new respect for the male ballet dancers who have to heave the ballerina about over their heads) or that she might hurt herself getting down or, of course, that we might be spotted . . . Oh, well, the girls have latchkeys these days and do as they please, not always with happy results. But it must make life simpler for their men friends.'

7

Discussions about the arrangements for the wedding soon gave John an opportunity to broach the subject of bridesmaids.

'Oh, I don't want that,' she said at once. 'When Simon and I were married, I just had my sister. She was already married, so she was technically a matron of honour. I don't see any reason to have anybody this time.'

'Would you reconsider that, darling, if I told you that Fred's little girls, Louise and Anne, are *dying* to be asked?'

She smiled.

'Are they really? Of course almost all little girls like being bridesmaids, or child attendants, whatever they are called. It is a chance to show off in public in a pretty dress and to feel important. And Louise and Anne are real poppets. Let me see – perhaps I could design something *very* simple that they would like to wear?'

'I'm sure you could. But don't bother yourself. It's only that Louise made me promise to speak to you about it.'

'Let me see,' she was evidently trying to visualize the effect. 'Perhaps they could be dressed in Regency costume – high waist, bonnets . . . ?'

'Jane Austen style?'

'Exactly.' She reached for her pencil, and drew the two children in the fancy dress she had suggested. 'Of course we should have to consult them and Mary . . . But they would look rather sweet like that? And we could have the same pink as my dress . . .'

John noted that she had already given way. It was agreed

that he would telephone Mary and, if she were favourable, send her Amanda's designs when she had worked them up.

These were diversions, in a period which was becoming extremely stressful for her and, in a way, even more for him. She at least was accustomed to the strain of waiting for the results of examinations and interviews. His own career had been almost carefree. Vicariously he suffered the torments of uncertainty all the more. And, as the date of her first London interview approached, he could hardly contain himself. He hoped for her sake, and still more for his own, that she would secure one of the appointments in the capital. He realized that they were exceedingly competitive.

'Would it make it less tiring for you if I *drove* you to the institute? . . .'

Amanda thought that it would make the wrong impression if she was seen arriving for the interview in her fiancé's sports car. But she was happy to be taken to the railway station.

'And what will you wear? The blue dress?'

She preferred to play for safety, in a linen suit.

'How will you do your hair? Up?'

'Yes,' she said. 'I am sure one ought to look as business-like as possible.'

But her best efforts could not disguise her beauty and attractiveness. He found himself wondering, at moments, whether he himself would not have had misgivings about employing a woman who looked like that. At other times, he felt that her seriousness of purpose *must* be apparent, if she were fairly interviewed, and he had no doubt that Professor Rogers had given her his full backing, though he did not know how influential the professor was with colleagues in London.

He arranged to meet her at the station after the interview. Provisionally, they agreed on a mid-afternoon train. As they did not know when she would finish, he realized that she might not catch it. He was disappointed, all the same, when she did not appear. He returned to the Lodgings. The Provost had, in the meantime, had a telephone call from her.

149

She had only just got away and feared that she would be too late to save John the trouble of a wasted journey to the station, but she had had no opportunity to ring up any earlier. The selection committee had seen her first and then asked her to wait while they saw other candidates; they had recalled her afterwards for what amounted to a second interview.

'Isn't that strange?' asked John.

'Somewhat unusual,' agreed his father.

'It must mean that she is in the running?'

'I think so. It may mean that the committee couldn't agree about her . . .'

'When do you suppose she'll know the result?' asked John, impatiently.

'If they are kind, someone might telephone this evening. Otherwise they'll simply write, in which case it won't be before the day after tomorrow.'

'Oh, damn. What's the time? The next train is not all that later, is it? I'll go and wait at the station.'

Eventually she came.

'It was curious,' she said, as he drove her back. 'It seemed to start quite well. The director, who was the chairman of the committee, began by asking me about my plans: whether you supported my wish to do a job, whether I could manage it, and so on. I suppose that was quite reasonable. And he seemed nice, John. Then he asked whether I had made any plans yet for research. I told them about the Burne-Jones window and showed them the photographs and drawings. I hadn't got very far with it, but I would expect to find out more about his methods of work and his relations with the people who commissioned these things, enough to make perhaps a short article, in due course. Then I got a lot of what I would call namby-pamby questions, patball. I didn't seem to get subjects that were really challenging.'

'And then they made you wait?'

'Yes. That was a bit unnerving. It seemed a long time. When they called me back, it was different. A man, who had asked only the most perfunctory things, did almost all the talking. He seemed rather hostile. But he raised interesting subjects. I began to enjoy it. Among other things, he asked me about English painters in the 1920s: who did I think was the most innovative? I said, Stanley Spencer. He asked me why. We discussed things like Spencer's use of perspective. Then he said, "Who else?" I suggested Nevinson . . . In the end, he left off. The director thanked me, very pleasantly, and said they would communicate with me as soon as possible.'

'Very unsatisfactory,' commented John.

He took her back to her flat. She was subdued, but did not seem to have lost heart.

About 9.00 there was a call from Professor Rogers.

'John Egerton? Good evening. I have a message for Mrs Orson. She doesn't seem to have a telephone of her own. Perhaps you could give it to her? It's confidential, so please keep it under your hat. You can tell the Provost of course.'

'Yes, yes. What is it?'

'The director rang me up a short time ago to say that she was going to be offered the job, subject to obtaining the diploma. And it would not be proper for me, as I shall be one of the examiners, to say that her success in that is a foregone conclusion, but I don't think she should worry too much.'

'That's splendid news. It's very kind of you to tell us. I'm sure she owes a great deal to your support.'

'Well, the director thought her much the most impressive of the candidates. One of his selection committee, quite an important man, refused to believe that a young woman who looked like that could be anything but a dilettante. When they had seen the other candidates, he was given a chance to interrogate her as he pleased, He expected that she would burst into tears. But she gave as good as she got.'

The Provost smiled when told.

'Burst into tears? She's not her father's daughter for nothing . . . Can you tell her tonight? Perhaps it's a bit late?'

John tried the telephone. There was no reply.

'That wretched communal telephone on the landing-depends on someone on that floor hearing it and answering. I shall go round.'

He hurried over to the flat and rang the bell.

After some moments, the door half-opened.

'Amanda darling, it's me. I have good news. A message for you from Professor Rogers. Can I come in?'

He entered to find her, somewhat flustered, with her hair in curlers and clad in a skimpy summer dressing gown which she had hastily flung round her.

'Sorry to intrude. I tried to telephone.'

'I wouldn't have heard it with the hairdryer on. Excuse me for receiving you like this.'

'You look sweet, as you always do. But I simply had to tell you.'

And he told her.

'That's marvellous,' she said. 'What splendid news, for us both. How good of you to make sure that I knew tonight. I shall sleep all the better. We must say goodnight now.'

He smiled at her. Feeling playful, he took her hand.

'Let me stay a little longer. It's still quite early . . .'

She coloured and disengaged her hand, stepping back.

'Don't say such a thing, John, even in fun. We shall see each other tomorrow.'

'As you wish, darling. At least, a goodnight kiss?'

She allowed the goodnight kiss.

Why did she have to be such a prude? he fumed as he went back to the Lodgings: old-fashioned, conventional, as his father had shrewdly said. For a few moments he could almost understand the exasperation of the handsome lecturer who had tried to seduce her and failed. Then he had to laugh at himself. He knew that he did not love her any the less on that account and, unlike his rivals, known and unknown, he could look forward to the triumph of possessing her with her willing consent.

He had begun negotiations, in the hope that they would be living in London, for a furnished flat which the owners wished to let for a year. They had reached a critical stage and he now lost no time in alerting Amanda.

'I heard of it through my grapevine. They are friends of friends. Mr Lloyd has to go abroad on business for twelve months and she is going with him. I have been to see it. They are anxious to get good tenants and I think I was acceptable. But they are leaving quite soon. If we don't finalize it now, they will accept some other offer.'

He showed her a plan of the flat. She studied it.

'Two bedrooms with bathroom, dressing room, a study, kitchen, sitting room, dining room . . . But a *large* dining room: look at the measurements. Surely we don't need that? Shan't we eat in the kitchen?'

'Certainly, when we're by ourselves. Not when we're giving a dinner party.'

'Are we going to give a dinner party?'

'Lots of them. I'm not going to be outdone by J.E. And I look forward to seeing my beautiful wife queening it at the opposite end of the table. I've checked: the dining room table will take twelve people.'

'Twelve? But how can I queen it and cook for that number of people, even if I had the skill?'

'I think we could look after four guests between us. When we plan something larger we'll use a firm of caterers. They only need lots of notice. If we book them soon, they should be able to do a party for Christmas.'

'I see. And are the Lloyds going to leave us china and glass? I've got enough for ourselves and you have probably too, but for twelve?'

'No. They want, understandably, to put their best things away in a locked cupboard. But J.E. is going to give us a dinner service, which we shall choose, and he has reserved some family silver spoons and forks for us. Fred and Mary have asked me what we want: I could say a canteen of knives. My partner, Mrs Howard, will probably be good for some glasses, if we ask her to the wedding. And we can hire, if necessary.'

'And tablecloths and napkins? And for that matter

blankets or duvets, sheets and towels . . . ? I have some of my trousseau still. And I'm sure Mummy would give me some things.'

'That's famous . . . Oh, by the way, they want us to look after their cat. Do you like cats?'

'It depends on the cat. Have you seen it?'

'Yes. It's a very pretty Siamese. Lovely blue eyes. Used to being thoroughly spoilt. Can't have kittens. I interviewed her. Or rather, she interviewed me. There was a lot of posturing and growling at first. But in the end she told her mistress that I might do.'

'That may be a nuisance. Still, if you like the flat . . . and if we can afford it . . .'

John told her the proposed rent. She whipped out a notebook and did a rapid calculation.

'I suppose that's not too bad for a whole year, and in London.'

'You've multiplied by twelve. Try multiplying by fifty-two.'

'*John!* It's not that per *week?*'

'Indeed it is. But don't panic. I've costed it very carefully. And let me show you. It's ideally placed for your place of work and for mine. And the block of flats has its own swimming bath and its own underground garages . . . We'll decide later on whether we want to go on living in that area or whether we want to move out to West Grove. Only, you must see it.'

'I would like to see it, of course. But if your really think it's all right, let's clinch it. You obviously know all about these things. I haven't time at the moment, with my exams coming on.'

'The fact is, my dear, the Lloyds *want* you to see it.'

'That's very nice of them, but . . .'

'They want to see *you*, in fact. I was incautious enough to mention your connection with the art world. I could tell at once that I had set alarm bells ringing. They associate artists with eccentricity, untidiness . . .'

'But that's absurd. They've met you. They must realize that

154

someone so smart and businesslike wouldn't be marrying a slut.'

'Smart and businesslike men can make fools of themselves in love like anyone else. I suspect they have visions of a woman who might spill paint or coffee over their pastel fitted carpets, make the washing machine seize up by stuffing crowds of dirty overalls into it, let the bath overflow, shut the cat into the deep-freeze, quarrel with the cleaners . . .'

'So I've got to come and convince them that I'm a reasonable housewife?'

'Well, aren't you? Your flat always looks spotless. Come on. Let's ring the Lloyds up. Going there will only take you away from your studies for a few hours . . .'

She accompanied him to the flat, which was on the sixth floor. Mr Lloyd opened the door.

'May I introduce you to my fiancée, Mrs Orson?'

'You may, indeed . . .'

John was beginning to accept the normal male reactions to meeting Amanda: surprise, admiration, benevolence . . . but he was particularly entertained to see how different she was to what they had expected.

In the sitting room, her attention was drawn to the window, and she went to it.

'Oh!' she exclaimed. 'The *river*. How *lovely*. John didn't tell me.'

Mrs Lloyd must have been used to hearing praise of the view, but she was none the less gratified.

She pointed out the landmarks on the opposite bank, and said, 'It is a constant source of pleasure to me. It changes all the time. The weather. The shipping. There is always something going on. Now, Mrs Orson, would you like me to show you the rest of the flat?'

They were gone quite a long time. When they came back, Amanda was holding the Siamese in her arms and it was purring loudly.

Mrs Lloyd said to her husband, 'Would you like to talk business now to Mr Egerton, dear?'

It was spoken so self-consciously that John realized it

must be a prearranged signal, intimating that she was satisfied.

The two men accordingly got down to signing both copies of the lease, which the Lloyds' solicitor had prepared.

Meanwhile Amanda's notebook, of which she had already filled several pages, was being completed with details of arrangements for cleaning, rubbish collection, tradesmen to be recommended or otherwise, neighbours on the same floor . . .

As they came away, she said thoughtfully, 'it is a *lovely* flat. I still think it is really too big for the two of us.'

'Two of us? But my dear, we are going to live there for a whole year after our wedding. Shan't we have a son or daughter living with us by the last two or three months, probably with a nanny in attendance?'

She looked sideways at him.

'No one can accuse you of not looking ahead, John.'

Some days later, Amanda received a letter from the widow, now remarried with two children, of Simon's navigator, with whom she had always kept in touch. She and another member of their circle were planning to have a requiem mass said at their parish church in London, on or near the anniversary of the disappearance of the aircraft. Now that formal confirmation of the crash had been recorded, they felt that some commemoration would be appropriate. Their present husbands, all RAF men themselves, approved. They hoped Amanda would come and, if rumours were correct that she had recently announced her engagement, that her fiancé would accompany her. And did she think that her father, as Simon's father-in-law and himself a distinguished pilot, would be willing to read a lesson?

'It will be ghastly,' she said, resignedly, 'But I must go. Sally is tip-top Anglo-Catholic and rather bossy. But she is efficient. It will be well-organized and there will be a reception afterwards in the parish room. Could you bear to come with me?'

'Of course I'll come, if you want me to,' answered John.

'What about your father? Have you spoken to him about it?'

'Yes, I have. He's not really keen, any more than I am, but he thinks we ought to go.'

'Good. I shall be glad of his moral support. I shall be utterly fish out of water.'

'And may I make the required contribution, it's quite a lot, on your account?'

'It's just as much your account as mine. You can do what you like with it. Won't this ceremony be terribly trying for you, though?'

'I can face it if you and Daddy are both there to support me . . .'

John thought that for him the occasion, though not trying, would be extremely dreary. In the end, it was not as bad as he feared.

The gathering of relatives and friends indeed looked few and forlorn to begin with, in the huge Victorian gothic church. But members of the choir gave as the anthem a creditable performance of part of Fauré's *Requiem* and the priest, Father James, delivered a short and quite eloquent sermon. He found the service unexpectedly moving. When Amanda's father moved out into the aisle to let her precede him to go up to the chancel, on impulse he got up and followed her.

As they came out of the church, while the organist thundered out the RAF march by way of voluntary, the air commodore, who had read the lesson in a fine parade ground voice, said in his ear, 'Well, I don't know whether all this ceremonial has done the poor chaps any good. At least it can't have done them any harm. I suppose they have better things to do than listen to us.'

'Such as?'

'You remember what Kipling wrote about the afterlife of artists? I've often quoted it to Amanda.'

'Quote it to me, please. I don't know my Kipling very well.'

His future father-in-law obliged.

And those that were good shall be happy: they shall
  sit in a golden chair;
They shall splash at a ten-league canvas with brushes
  of comets' hair;
They shall find real saints to draw from – Magdalene,
  Peter, and Paul;
They shall work for an age at a sitting, and never be
  tired at all.

'What would the equivalent be for an airman?'
'I can't imagine. I'm not a poet. But I suppose the
Almighty can find things to do for everyone who is good at
their work.'
'And Simon was good at it?'
'Oh, yes. A nice quiet chap. Only interested in his work
– and in Amanda. He was an outstanding pilot. He talked
to me about changing to commercial flying later on. He
wanted to be able to give Amanda everything. He could have
earned a lot of money as a test pilot. A dangerous profession.
But not more dangerous than war. I have known test pilots
who survived to retire. Now we must go and make ourselves
agreeable to the company . . .'
This proved an uphill task for John. In the end, he took
refuge with the parson. He told him of Amanda's interests
in art history. There was an instant response. Father James
turned out to be an enthusiast. When Amanda joined them,
there was a learned and animated discussion.
'The church itself is Pugin, of course. But the original
windows in the lady chapel, which you haven't seen, I expect,
were so badly damaged by a fire some years later that they
had to be replaced, and for that the parish went to William
Morris.'
'Isn't that exciting?' said Amanda. 'We are coming to live
in London when we are married and I shall look forward
to seeing the lady chapel then.'
'Let me give you my card. And please don't fail to get in
touch with me when you come. It would be a pleasure to
show you round. We have some records about them, too,

though I fear they are incomplete. Few people have felt any interest in them or in their history.'

John found a letter awaiting him at St Matthew's from Richard and Sue. The dance club to which they belonged, and of which Richard was now vice-president, was going to celebrate its fiftieth anniversary with a gala ball, a white tie occasion. A really good band. A champagne supper. And so on. Each member could invite a pair of guests. Would John and Amanda like to come? If so, would it be acceptable as their wedding present? They could spend the night if they didn't mind cramped conditions. Amanda could have the boys' room; Paul would be away camping, and Jamie was going to Sue's mother for the night. John could share Richard's dressing room and sleep on the sofa bed in the lounge.

Amanda was delighted. Then she had what John had come to call one of her 'panics'.

'Everyone there will be terribly expert. I haven't danced for several years. I shall be out of practice, out of date, I shall let you down.'

John solved that one without too much difficulty. Why shouldn't they have some dancing lessons together, to brush up their skills? He was himself, he said, not quite truthfully, almost equally out of practice. Amanda agreed. After making a few inquiries, they made an appointment with a teacher. She was cooperative.

After a few rehearsals of conventional dances, she suggested, 'What about Ceroc? Very up to date . . .'

'What's that?' inquired Amanda.

'It's a jive. I've done it in France. Will you risk it? It's fun . . .'

'I'll risk any dance with you . . .'

Meanwhile she had remembered that she no longer had a dance-dress. But her exams would be over by then, and a shopping expedition to London was already planned.

'Better and better. Oh, what fun, dressing Amanda. What pleasures to look forward to.'

She was up in arms.

159

'You talk as if I were a doll,' she said, pettishly.

'Do I? How would I know? Boys don't have dolls. At least, they didn't in my time. Anything may happen these days. And I didn't have sisters. I only know that I have an enchantress who looks more bewitching every fresh thing I see her wearing.'

'What a plausible flatterer you are.'

But she was mollified. She was not usually so touchy, he thought, and he realized that it might be attributed to nerves at the approach of her examinations.

In fact she sailed through them with the minimum of trouble and had the satisfaction of hearing the result quickly, as there were few candidates.

So they both felt exceptionally carefree when they set out for the dance, having had a shopping spree in London which included a ravishing ball dress.

They were prepared for an enjoyable evening, but it exceeded their expectations. The standard of the dancing was high and, as John had anticipated, a samba with Sue was quite an experience.

Richard was, initially, startled at the suggestion of a Ceroc.

'Of course, Sue and I have done it. It's very jolly. But at a formal dance?'

He consulted the president and his wife, who said, 'Too strenuous for us. But I'm sure the younger members of the club would enjoy it.'

'And why not?' exclaimed Sue. 'Aren't we told that all the fashionable dances, minuets, mazurkas and what-not, began as popular ones?'

Richard agreed.

'And I'll have someone call out the steps, as in a country dance. Some people may not know them.'

'Always nice to be reminded,' agreed John.

He and Amanda made a few mistakes, but it did not seem to matter and it added spice to the occasion.

The morning after, John woke to find that it was already 10.00. He got up, washed and dressed and restored the sofa on which he had slept to its original state. There was almost no sound in the house. But on investigating he found his hostess, who had just come down, in the kitchen.

'Oh, you're bright and early, John,' she said. 'I'm just going to make breakfast for us.'

'Nothing like a splendid supper for giving one an appetite, is there? Can I help, Sue? I can make eggs and bacon, or sausages. And coffee . . .'

At that moment, Richard came in, followed almost at once by Amanda.

'Darling, just think,' said Sue. 'John has offered to make breakfast. I for one shan't refuse such a good offer. I'll get eggs and bacon out. Here's the frying pan. Would anyone like cereals first? Amanda, shall we lay the table and make coffee, or tea if you prefer? Dick, be an angel and make the toast and warm the plates . . .'

They sat down to an ample feast.

'I see you're an accomplished bachelor, John,' she commented. 'Amanda will be almost out of a job, won't she? Do you always have a cooked breakfast when you are on your own?'

'Always. You see, I have nearly always been first for a swim, and been out before my workmen to get them started.'

'All that before going to the office?'

'That's right. Then I usually just have sandwiches for lunch.'

'But you have a proper dinner?'

'Oh, yes. I tend to go out for dinner. But it will be for Amanda to say. And talking of dinner, what a gorgeous entertainment we had last night. And they're fine rooms. Are they your own premises?'

'We share them with the local social club,' said Richard. 'It works very well. The membership overlaps.'

'Nice as it is,' observed Sue, 'I think there is nothing so nice as a dance in a private house. Of course that is rare nowadays. Sometimes there is a ball after a wedding, which is great fun. But it is usually in the marquee. Now, I so much enjoyed, in the TV performance of *Pride and Prejudice*,

161

watching the characters dance in the parlour of somebody's house, was it Mr Bingley's?, just to a piano and a fiddle if I remember right, by candlelight – so pretty.'

'Doesn't Jane Austen say something amusing about dancing, in one of the novels?' volunteered Amanda.

'I don't remember it in *Pride and Prejudice*,' replied Sue. 'But I suppose they left a lot of things out in the TV version.'

'"I think it's in *Emma*,' said Amanda.

'Oh, I've got *Emma*,' said Sue, at once. 'I bought a copy when they said it would be the next to be televised. I must admit I haven't read it yet. Do look up the place.'

The paperback was duly produced and Amanda, nothing loath, found the passage and read it aloud to the others.

'"It may be possible to do without dancing entirely. Instances have been known of young people passing many, many months successively, without being at a ball of any description, and no material injury accrue either to body or mind, but when a beginning is made – when the felicities of rapid motion have once been, though slightly, felt – it must be a very heavy set that does not ask for more."'

'Oh, that's capital,' said Richard. 'I must bring it in to my next speech at the club.'

John smiled at her.

'I didn't know that you were a Janeite among your many other accomplishments, darling.'

Sue meantime had come down to earth.

'I mustn't forget, I have to go and collect Jamie. He is with my mother, Amanda. She loves having him, but he wears her out if he is there too long. Will you come with me? It is only a few streets away.'

Amanda willingly agreed.

'But we must help you put these things away first . . .'

'I'll do that,' said Richard, at once. 'They only have to be shoved into the dishwasher. Perhaps John might give me a hand.'

Sue and Amanda set off and the two men disposed rapidly

of the washing up and then sat down on the sofa with the Sunday papers. They exchanged some comments on the business news.

After a few minutes, they returned to the subject of the dance. John was genuinely impressed.

'The committee did a marvellous job. Everything went like clockwork. It was the greatest fun.'

'Amanda was the belle of the ball,' responded Richard. 'And she is so sweet and modest with it. She quite won my heart. And she is a pleasure to dance with. She said she was out of practice, but one would hardly have noticed it. She has a lovely sense of rhythm and her footwork is beautifully neat.'

John returned the compliment.

'Sue is a marvellous partner. I had expected that. Because, among other reasons, J.E. told me what fun he had dancing with her at the St Matthew's function.'

'That's right,' said Richard. 'He danced with her twice. She had been rather nervous. Rather overawed, you know. She didn't know the university world. But they got on famously. The second time, he asked her for a tango. Did you know J.E. could tango?'

'No, but I would have assumed he could. It was still smart when he and Mama were first going to dances.'

'Of course, when we were children they went to dances quite a lot. Mama had the most marvellous dresses, didn't she? And lovely scent. And fairy-tale jewellery . . .'

John looked thoughtfully at his brother.

'Did J.E. ever tell you about that dance they went to before they were married? When she was still at school?'

'No. I never heard about that.'

John told him.

Richard was delighted. He slapped his thigh.

'Bravo, Mama. And bravo, J.E. I must say, though, I'm glad none of my girlfriends ever asked me to do anything so risky. J.E. always does things in style. How splendid he was at that party we got up for his fifty-fifth birthday . . . Oh, you weren't there, John. Something happened. Fred

organized it and he said you hadn't answered the invitation.'
Richard looked at his brother in perplexity.

'I couldn't come,' said John, quickly. 'To tell you the truth, I didn't want to. But I should have answered, of course. Then Fred made things worse by coming to my flat and making an awful scene.'

'You didn't want to?' Richard said, slowly. 'I suppose, John, you really hardly *knew* J.E.? Fred and I were with him a great deal when we were boys. When *you* were growing up, he was away a lot. He was at a crucial stage of his career. Often abroad. Often working late at the office. And you were spending the vacations mostly in France with Henri.'

'You're right. He seemed very remote. Partly my fault . . .'

Anxious to change the subject, he came back to last night's dance.

'I must tell you how much I admired Sue's dress. I thought that emerald colour suited her so well. She resists the temptation to be very décolletée . . . ?' He had in fact been surprised at the style: a high neck and three-quarter sleeves. He would have expected something more daring.

Richard's face clouded over.

'She *has* to.' He hesitated. 'She has the marks of an old injury on her back which she feels it would be disagreeable for other people to have to look at.'

'I'm so sorry. An accident . . . ?'

'If I tell you how it really happened, John, will you keep it to yourself? It is nothing to be ashamed of. But it is extremely painful, I haven't told anyone on our side of the family. Not even J.E.'

'Of course. Please don't tell me unless you want to. I shan't say anything.'

'No. I shall. I think it would be a relief.'

Richard bent forward, his face in his hands, and began, in a low voice.

'Sue's first husband ill-treated her almost from the beginning. He drank and it got worse. Then, one evening, he came home drunk and violent. She was ironing his shirts. He picked a quarrel with her. He knocked her down. He

164

was a big man. And he took the hot iron and attacked her with it. She still has the scars all over her back and shoulders.'

'Good God!'

'She was in hospital for several weeks. They did wonders for her, she said, but there was a limit to what they could do mitigate the unsightliness. When she came out, she went to live with her mother. She got a divorce, eventually. The bank, where she had worked, thought highly of her and took her back. And she rejoined the dance club, which had been her great hobby, I joined it about the same time, I met her there. We were both on our own. We danced together several times. She was wonderful. I fell in love with her. When I proposed, she told me she was divorced. And she said there was something else she must tell me before I committed myself. It was this disfigurement, as she called it. Of course, it made no difference. But I didn't realize until I saw it *how* dreadful it was. Oh John . . . her beautiful body . . . to treat her like that . . . the brute . . .'

Instinctively John put his arm round his brother, who was struggling with tears.

'A husband from Hell,' he said. 'It's wonderful that it hasn't scarred her for life psychologically. It shows what a brave woman she is.'

'Yes, doesn't it?' said Richard, eagerly. 'She still has nightmares about it. Less often, now. When that happens, I almost despair. I lie in bed and think however can I make up to her all she has been through? I do try . . .'

He clutched John's hand.

'But Richard, you have done everything humanly possible. You have given her your love and a nice home and two jolly kids. What more could any man do?'

'Do you really think so?'

'Of course. Sue couldn't look as happy as she does if you hadn't made her happy.'

'How comforting you are, John.' Richard dried his eyes. 'You *have* cheered me up. Strange. You used to be a little demon who didn't care a damn about anyone else – except Mama.'

'One grows up.'

'And then, there's that angelic girl. She would humanize *anyone*. She'd tame tigers.'

John smiled.

'I have exactly the opposite problem to you, with her. Amanda's first husband was her dream man. First love. Love at first sight. A cult object. I've got to live with this. And try to live up to it.'

Richard was reassuring in his turn.

'I had a talk with her when we were sitting out after our second dance together. Apparently she met *him* at a dance? But she seems to have taken you on in good earnest.'

They had agreed that they might spend the afternoon looking at houses in one of the areas which John had decided to target in his next property transactions. He had secured the keys from the agents, who knew him well. And after a quick lunch at a roadside pub they set off. The first two properties were of the kind he had regularly repaired and modernized. One at least proved to be quite eligible. Amanda was dismayed at first by its state. He explained how he would tackle it. She began to see it through his eyes. The third house, which was at the corner of the same street, called West Grove, was a good deal larger and had extensive grounds. It was extremely attractive, at first glance. On closer inspection it was evident that it had not been lived in for a number of years, or even looked at by a prospective purchaser. A rambler rose, intended to frame the doorway, had collapsed and had to be pulled to one side to gain entry. Indoors all was dark. After some fumbling John found the switch. Reluctantly, a feeble centre light came on. They began to explore the house. The floorboards creaked under their footsteps. The hinges whined as they opened the doors. Everything was covered in dust. Some of the windows had been boarded up, as if to defend them against vandals. Elsewhere the ancient Virginia creeper which covered the outside walls had intruded and blocked the light. Swarms of flies buzzed frenziedly against the dirty glass.

166

They entered the derelict parlour. As their eyes became accustomed to the dim light, they were able to make out a big room with good proportions, a handsome fireplace, and elegant panelling. There were shutters, which John opened with some difficulty, to reveal a view of the garden, a jungle of a garden. What had once been a lawn was a hayfield. The rose garden beyond was a tangled mass of weeds in which the few surviving bushes struggled to show a few blooms. Beyond, the place was a wilderness, in which rhododendrons rampaged unchecked, smothering whatever other shrubs there might be. Only two magnificent wellingtonias, no doubt planted when the house was built, rose defiantly above the chaos.

'There would be room for a swimming pool over there,' John pointed out to her. 'It's at least a hectare. Over two acres.' And here,' he kicked the dust, 'this is real parquet flooring. Just the thing for that dance Sue was talking about, eh?'

It had clearly been a charming place. They both liked it enormously. Completing their inspection, they went through the dining room and pantry, into the kitchen.

'It's a good big room,' she commented. 'And a fine walk-in larder on the north-east corner. Do you feel, John? Even today it's quite cool. And there would be plenty of room for a fridge and a freezer. And I suppose this smaller room was a sort of scullery. Leading to the back door. But the kitchen's got a miserable outlook. Just onto the garage and out-houses.'

John smiled.

'There were servants in the kitchen then, dear. They were not meant to spy on their employers disporting themselves out of doors. Look, we should only have to knock a hole in this south wall, and put a nice window in and you would have the view over the garden.'

They retraced their steps and surveyed the house again from outside.

'Pretty? Pretty enough to make a love nest for us darling?'

'I think it's enchanting. The best kind of early Victorian.

It has great character. A friendly character. Do you really think that it could be made habitable?'

'As long as it hasn't got dry rot in it. I don't see any sign of that. But we'll have a proper survey done. If it's all right, we'll buy the place. We shall get it cheap. Of course, we shall have to spend nearly as much again to restore and modernize it.'

Amanda tried to be practical.

'What about transport into London? It seems the other end of everywhere.'

'Five minutes walk to the Underground. I wouldn't look at a house otherwise.'

'It seems a rather sleazy neighbourhood. What sort of neighbours would we have?'

'It won't be sleazy for long once I have got to work on re-habilitating it. We've already got our eye on one other house in the same street, haven't we? And if we're not satisfied with it, we can always sell it to someone else and try again.'

As they were about to get into the car, John noticed an adjoining house, just beyond the garage. He remarked to Amanda that it looked as if it had once been part of the same group of buildings.

'You are quite right,' she said, studying attentively what they could see of it. 'And it looks like the work of the same architect as the house, only much smaller.'

'Might have been a gardener's cottage, or a chauffeur's,' suggested John. 'Shall we reconnoitre it?'

'Why? Is it for sale?' she asked.

'Not that I know of. But it would be an asset to the house, wouldn't it? Shall we go and call on the people there?'

'Complete strangers . . . ?'

'If they're out, we can at least see what it looks like from the street. If they shut the door in our faces, we're no worse off. Give me my panama, darling, in case there's a lady there.'

The little house, which had a name, West Grove Lodge, as well as a street number, was a complete contrast to the main house. The garden was neat and colourful, the woodwork freshly painted, and there were dainty chintz curtains in the windows.

John rang the bell. After a few moments, there was the sound of footsteps. The door opened, as far as a safety chain would allow, and a woman's face peered out, surprised and suspicious.

He took his hat off and said, 'Excuse us for disturbing you. My fiancée and I have been looking over the house next door, West Grove. We like it very much and we intend to buy it and do it up, to live in ourselves. As we shall be neighbours, if that succeeds, we have taken the liberty of calling.'

She undid the chain and opened the door wide.

'You have been looking at West Grove?' she said, incredulously. 'It is almost a ruin.'

'It is in a bad state. You are quite right,' he answered. 'But I have a good deal of experience of restoring such houses. And we have really fallen in love with this place. And the garden could be lovely . . .'

She looked from him to Amanda. She seemed reassured. 'Won't you come in?'

Inside, everything was spotless, but her tiny parlour was cluttered with an immense number of knick-nacks, china ornaments and photographs. Among the latter, he noticed one of the garden at West Grove, recognizable by the two wellingtonias.

'Oh, yes,' she said, following his gaze. 'That's the garden as it used to be. My father used to be the head gardener. It's a sad sight now.'

With a little encouragement, she brought out a group of the staff as it had been some time in the 1920s: a chauffeur, in uniform, three gardeners and a boy, in cloth caps, striped shirts and waistcoats, the cook, parlour maid, and a couple of housemaids in frilly white caps and aprons.

'That's my father,' she said, pointing to one of the gardeners, 'and that's my mother,' indicating a young housemaid. 'She used to give a hand in the house before she was married.'

169

'And this house belongs to you now, Miss . . . ?'

'Perkins. Doris Perkins. No,' she said. 'It still belongs like the big house to Mrs Millett. She is over 90 now and lives in a nursing home. Her husband and her son were both killed in the war. She did not want to go on living there. She let it. The tenants did not look after it. In the end she decided to sell it. No one bought it . . . And now she has given up spending any money on it. But she let my mother and me go on living here and she pays for any work that needs doing. My mother died last year.'

'So you live here alone, Miss Perkins?' asked Amanda.

'Yes, but,' answering the unspoken question, 'I am not lonely. I go out to work. The ladies are very good to me. They're not nearby, of course. This neighbourhood has gone down dreadfully.'

Amanda asked about shops.

There were a few, rather humble ones, at one end of the next street. There was still a post office. And there was a supermarket, not within walking distance, but accessible by car or even by bicycle. Miss Perkins was sometimes given a lift there by friends.

And a church?

There was St Margaret's quite close.

'Not many of us go,' lamented Miss Perkins. 'And the vicar doesn't live in the vicarage now. It was sold several years ago. He comes to take the services. I'm sure he does his best. He has two other parishes to look after.'

She and Amanda agreed that this was a general problem nowadays.

John judged that the right stage of cautious good relations had been reached.

He produced his business card.

'If all goes well, Miss Perkins, we shall start doing up West Grove in about a month's time. I'm afraid there may be some disturbance. Workmen's cars, builders' lorries, arriving early in the morning. But they are decent men, known personally to me. They won't be more of a nuisance than they can help.'

170

Miss Perkins took the card and looked at it.

'Thank you, sir,' she said. 'I shall be glad to see the house taken in hand.'

'And don't you think,' he said to Amanda, when they had left, 'that we'll try to get Mrs Millett to sell us the cottage as well as the house? We'll undertake to let Doris Perkins continue to live there on the same terms. She might even be useful to us. While we're about it, shall we see if John Wilkin, my builder, is in, and tell him about it? I haven't been in touch with him for over a year but we might try. Sure you're not tired?'

They made their way to the 1950's housing estate where the builder lived.

'He may be asleep as it's a Sunday afternoon. Do you mind waiting in the car while I enquire? It's in the shade . . .'

He rang the bell. After a few moments, Mrs Wilkin came to the door.

'Mr Egerton? Well, I never. We didn't know what had happened to you. Come in. I'll call my hubby. He's in the garden.'

Mr Wilkin came in, saying cheerfully, 'Glad to see you. We thought you was dead.'

John told him about the houses and asked whether he would be free to work on them, with his partner, if the risk of dry rot was eliminated. Mr Wilkin had a little job during the school holidays, doing some repairs to the local primary school for the council. He had nothing after that.

'Would you want it finished by a particular date for someone?'

'We can talk about that. I have in mind to live in West Grove myself. I'm going to be married soon.'

Congratulations were offered.

'Stay and have a cup of tea with us.'

'Very kind of you. No. I mustn't. I have my fiancée waiting in the car.'

Wouldn't the young lady like to come in?

John went out to ask Amanda whether she would care to meet them ('Rather rough and ready . . .') She got out at

171

once and came in with him. Introductions were effected. Mrs Wilkin turned to put the kettle on. Then some little Wilkins, who had been playing in the garden, came in. They stared at Amanda for a moment, open-mouthed. She smiled at them, and said 'Hello.' They needed no further invitation.

Mrs Wilkin expostulated, as she brought the tea, 'Mind the lady's dress, there . . . sticky fingers . . .'

But as well discourage flies from honey. Amanda already had the smallest one on her lap and the next was climbing up her. She wanted to know their names, their ages . . .

Mr Wilkin had paid the tribute of some admiring glances in her direction. But he was anxious to do business with John.

'And you was going to rebuild a house somewhere abroad? France, wasn't it?'

'That's right. That was what took the time. It was a big job. And they were slow about getting it finished.'

'Them Frenchmen weren't used to being hurried like you've always hurried us, I wouldn't wonder,' said Wilkin, with a grin. 'I take it they're a lazy lot. Now, shall I have a word with the carpenter? We could get going when the school holidays are over, that's early September.'

They both pencilled the date in their diaries and exchanged up to date addresses and telephone numbers.

Then farewells were said.

On the way home. Amanda reverted to the subject of the ball.

'How nice Richard and Sue are and how kind they were to me. Do you know, I thought Richard was rather quiet, I don't mean dull, of course, but he's quite different on the dance floor. Great fun, in fact. More like you . . .'

The next morning John plunged into intense activity, telephoning house agents and solicitors, arranging for structural surveys, submitting requests for planning permission.

He spent most of the week in London following this up. He was determined to make no mistakes this time. Hitherto he had relied on a natural flair for estimating costs. Now he would be more painstaking. And he decided to allocate only a certain proportion of his capital to these building projects and to invest the remainder in more conventional ways. He even consulted Mrs Howard about this. She was clearly a little flattered, and went into the plans with great care. As if to seal their reconciliation, she asked him to dinner at her flat the following Sunday.

She had also invited Kitty Williams and her boyfriend and another young couple. It was an excellent dinner, although she made them very late by serving an elaborate menu; she was singlehanded, and disdained well-meant offers of help from the younger women, so there were long intervals between courses, and it was almost midnight when they had coffee. He escaped before one o'clock.

Her flat was not well-placed for parking, and he had left the car in a quiet square some distance away. As he began to walk back, he thought with satisfaction about the events of the week. The dance had been the real highlight. Amanda had looked marvellous. Dancing with her was wonderful. Even staying with Sue and Richard had been unexpectedly rewarding. The drama that lay behind their sedate suburban existence had rendered them much more interesting to him. And then, the return to his true business enthusiasm greatly excited him, particularly the restoration of West Grove.

He planned to take the same short cut to the square as he had used on his arrival. It went through some old mews, now housing low-grade garages and mean workshops. At night, it looked less attractive. It was ill-lit, and faint moonlight only had the effect of making it look dingier still. With instincts sharpened by considerable experience of London after dark, he stopped and decided to go the longer way round by a main street.

Then he heard a cry for help. He ran forward. At first he thought someone had fallen. As he got closer, he saw that a passer-by was being attacked by two masked men. The assailants, fully occupied with their victim, were at first unaware of his approach. They seemed to be trying to force something over his mouth and they had a rope. A kidnap rather than a mugging?

John shouted, 'Lay off, you bastards.'

And, as the man nearest him looked round, he summoned what he could remember of the boxing skills which he had been taught at school and landed a punch which brought him down.

The other man turned on him with a curse. John saw the flash of steel, and grabbed his wrist, trying to wrest the weapon from him. There was a furious struggle. Then his opponent managed to get his arm partly free for a moment, though not sufficiently to aim with accuracy, and the blade of the knife struck the side of his head. He felt a sudden searing pain. Blood spurted into his eye and began to pour down his face. He staggered back and fell heavily against the kerb.

8

Fragments and phantoms of his main preoccupations in recent years flapped round him like pieces of old newspaper blown about in a neglected street. Aimlessly. Inexorably. Market quotations, estimates, reports from surveyors, letters from planning committees, rents, insurance, income tax, invitations, programmes ... Trivial, tawdry, inconsequent ... He tried to shake them off, in vain.

'Wherever this is, I must get out of here. Out ...'

And then, answering the last word, a phrase came uppermost in his mind like an illuminated sign, a phrase which he had heard in the requiem for Simon Orson and his colleagues.

'Out of the deep ...'

At once, he heard his name being called, at an immense distance, but very insistently.

'John. John. John.'

He struggled to respond.

The voice seemed to come nearer.

He tried again.

He became aware that he was in pain. He heard himself give a little moan. He opened his eyes.

The voice, which he now recognized, said, 'Well done. Brave boy.'

A blur of white came slowly into focus. He was in bed and his father was beside him.

'J.E.? Where am I?'

'You're in hospital in London, in a private room. You had a go at two thugs on Sunday night and were injured.'

He tired to sort out his recollections.

'That's right. One of them knifed me. Is Amanda all right? She wasn't with me, was she?'

'No, you were alone, walking back from Mrs Howard's flat. Amanda is here. She has a room in a hotel close to the hospital. She has been very anxious about you.'

'Can you let her know that I am all right?'

The Provost looked at his watch.

'I certainly will. I'll leave it until a bit later, if you don't mind. It's only half past six. I insisted on her going to the hotel last night to try to get a proper night's sleep. She had been sitting up with you for hours.'

He puzzled over this.

'Half past six? In the morning? What time did you come, then?'

'I've been here all night. Amanda and I arranged that one of us would be here all the time. We wanted to make sure that you wouldn't be alone when you regained consciousness. It has taken quite a long time. You were concussed, of course. Are you in much pain, John?'

'My head hurts. Everything hurts.'

'I'll see if I can find a nurse. They ought to be able to give you something to relieve it. Then I shall go to my club and get some sleep. And ring up Amanda first. She is due to come in later this morning.'

'Could you give me a drink of water? I feel thirsty.'

His father held a glass to his lips and he drank. Then, overcome with a great lassitude, he went to sleep.

When he woke up, a young nurse was attending to him. He asked her what she was called.

She said, 'Anthea.'

'What a nice name. It means a flower, doesn't it?'

'They tell me so. And you've got some lovely flowers. Have you seen them?'

He had vaguely noticed something brightly coloured beyond the foot of the bed.

'No, I haven't.'

'Wouldn't you like to look at them?'

176

And without waiting for an answer she began to bring over a succession of flowers and to read aloud, with a certain avidity, the messages that accompanied them. First came some magnificent pink lilies, 'From Fred, Mary and the children, with best wishes for your recovery.'

Flowers from Fred. How ludicrous.

And there were red roses from Richard and Sue, Paul and Jamie. Then there were white roses from Amanda's father and mother. And pink carnations from Betsy Howard.

'And there are some "Get well" cards . . .'

'Oh, don't bother. I'll look at them later. My head hurts. Everything hurts.'

'You've quite a bad cut on your head and a bit of a fracture of the skull. And bruising.'

'What does the cut look like? Can you show me?'

After a few minutes' search she found a hand mirror.

He looked at his reflection, incredulous.

'What's that thing coming down my forehead?'

'That's the cut. Right down to within an inch of the eyebrow. Lucky it wasn't your eye.'

'It looks horrible. Will it take long to heal?'

'Oh, no. Two weeks from now at most. The fracture will take a bit longer. About four weeks, I think. You may have a scar, but it won't show much.'

'And what has happened to my hair?'

'They'll have had to shave it off to get at the injuries.'

'What a damn nuisance. I'm getting married in a few weeks. It couldn't grow again as quickly as that.'

Anthea took more interest.

'You could get a wig. You can get one on the NHS. Ask your GP.'

John was not unduly dismayed by the idea of a wig. He had worn one frequently on the stage. But he was beginning to be troubled by the immediate effect of his appearance on Amanda.

'At least we could get rid of this horrid stubble. My fiancée will be coming in this morning. Could you shave me?'

'I could. I haven't time, though.'

'Please do, Anthea. I'm sure you wouldn't want *your* pretty face scratched by bristles like this.'

She relented.

'I'll see what I can do.'

A few minutes later she reappeared and shaved him. It was not at all comfortable, but it served its purpose.

'You're very dark, aren't you? Actually, you'd look rather good with a beard . . .'

He began to come out of his next sleep with a pleasurable sensation, although he still felt pain. At first he was uncertain which sense was giving it to him. Was it the thought of a picture? a piece of music? a delicious taste? and then he became aware that it was a scent. Amanda's perfume. He opened his eyes. She was beside him.

'Darling John, how marvellous to see you awake and with a little colour in your cheeks.'

'I'm afraid it's an ugly sight, my dear. And I'm as weak as a kitten.'

'Some kitten. He'll soon be a tiger again.'

Uneasily, he attempted a joke.

'You're concentrating on communicating with the person?'

'As if I needed to. I'm enjoying looking at your dear face and your lovely violet eyes.'

'Could you bear to give me a kiss, then?'

The kiss was only interrupted by the arrival of the trolley with the patients' lunch.

'Shall I help you?' she asked.

As she seemed to want to, he agreed, though the smell of boiled fish was dispiriting.

She sampled it and reported, 'Not at all bad.'

She took a spoonful and held it carefully to his mouth. He nibbled, gingerly, at first finding the process a little humiliating. Then he saw a smile playing round her lips and some appetite began to return. He remembered from some of his light-hearted love affairs, that feeding one another could be at least marginally part of the fun. Now, in the

178

unpromising setting of the hospital room, it was creating a new intimacy between them, even though, for the moment, it was she who had to make the running. His standing in her eyes became a less pressing preoccupation. He smiled at her and ate docilely.

'This kitten finds every morsel a bowl of cream, because it comes from you. Now you must excuse me: I feel snoozy.'

'Yes, do sleep. It will do you good. I shall go and have some lunch in the canteen.'

When he woke he felt slightly more active. He asked her how she had heard of his accident, when she had come to London . . .

'Your father telephoned me at 8.30 on Monday morning,' she replied. 'He explained and asked me to join him here as soon as I could. They had rung him up at 2.30 in the night, as his name and address had been found on you.'

'But how monstrous, to knock him up at that hour.'

'They thought you might not live until the morning, John. You had nearly bled to death when help reached you.'

'Good Heavens. I was as bad as that?'

'Yes, indeed. So naturally I came up by the next train, with things for the night as he had advised. I met him as arranged outside intensive care. We arranged that we would take it in turns to be with you. So I went in . . . It was terrible. You were as white as a sheet, hardly breathing – having blood transfusions, of course. I whispered to one of the nurses, "How is he?" She said, "I'm afraid it's touch and go, dear. He's fighting for his life." So I just sat down and shut my eyes and prayed.'

'You must be very prayer-effective, darling.'

'Oh, I'm sure your father was praying, too.'

'Has he gone back to St Matthew's now?'

'Yes. He had left messages for his secretary, of course, to inform the college.'

'And someone told Fred and Richard, and Betsy Howard.'

'Yes. I think he did.'

There was a pause.

179

'Tell me about yourself, darling. Are you comfortable at the hotel? Can you get meals there? And, by the way, are you all right for money?'

'Oh, yes, thank you. How sweet of you to think of it. I have the card, you know. It has been a godsend.'

'That reminds me. I don't know what has happened to my wallet. I suppose those rogues pinched it. We must report it . . .'

'No, don't worry. The police found it intact. They gave it to your father when he contacted them on Monday. They thought the criminals were in a hurry to leave: the man you rescued, John, had got away and they knew he had probably gone to raise the alarm.'

'I'm glad he was all right. And my clothes . . . They were a write-off?'

'Not quite. I tracked them down in the hospital, and took your suit to the cleaners. In my home town, they would have fainted at the sight of all that blood and dirt. In London nobody turned a hair. They said they couldn't guarantee that no marks would be left, but they were sure they could make it wearable. I am due to collect it this afternoon.'

'A good thing I didn't wear that light grey suit, as I thought of doing. And my watch? It claims to be waterproof and shockproof, but I expect it was broken?'

'Your father has it. I believe the glass was cracked. He is having it seen to.'

'And the *car*, darling! Joyriders have probably done it in by now.'

'No. Your father knew the make and number and whereabouts you were likely to have left it. The police traced it on Monday.'

'Well, I seem to have got off pretty lightly. *You* must have had the most dreadful time. You and J.E.'

'Nothing matters as long as you are all right.'

Anthea helped him to have breakfast the following morning, after which he dozed off.

A different nurse woke him, saying, 'Dr Croft is just

coming. He asks whether you would mind if he brings some students with him.'

'Why should I mind?' he grunted, sleepily. 'Let 'em all come.'

After a few moments, a tall middle-aged man came into the room, followed by a girl and three or four young men, all wearing white coats. He spoke briefly to John and then gave the others a short account of what had happened. The injuries were quite banal, of the kind which frequently came into casualty on a Saturday night: a knife wound to the head, causing a slight fracture of the skull, concussion, loss of blood, bruises ... But the consultant was in a pedagogic mood. He turned back the bed-clothes, and told the young man nearest him to describe the damage. The student began glibly with the cut and the bruises. But he was quickly interrupted.

'I want a scientific description. Such as you would pass to another hospital, or to the patient's GP.'

The young man did his best. When he paused for a moment, trying to remember the correct anatomical term, Dr Croft cocked an eyebrow at one of the others, who gleefully supplied it.

Then he opened another line of enquiry.

'The patient fell against a kerb or low wall, evidently on his left side, to judge by the bruising, as you said. But there are also three separate bruises on his right side. Do they look the same?'

They all peered at them. One of the students said, 'No, sir. I would have said they're more like the bruises we sometimes see after a rugger match.'

'Which are caused by ... ?'

'Usually by a kick.'

'Well, the patient hasn't been playing rugger. So how would he have got them?'

'During the fight, perhaps?'

This time, it was at John himself that the eyebrow was cocked.

He said, simply, 'No.'

'After it, then?'

'Might have been. I'd passed out by then. They might well have been vexed. After all, I'd spoilt their game, and given one of them a crack on the jaw.'

'Which accounts for the bruise on your knuckles?'

John grinned.

'I suppose so. Bare fists, you know. No time to observe Queensberry rules.'

But the girl said, indignantly, 'They kicked him when he was lying unconscious? What *brutes.*'

He smiled at her.

Dr Croft seemed to decide that the conversation was becoming insufficiently clinical. He turned to go.

John said, hastily, 'Please tell me. How soon shall I be back to normal?'

'The fracture should heal in four weeks. You will probably get headaches, and bouts of weakness for longer. Call it six weeks to be back to normal.'

'Six weeks? But I'm being married on 25 July.'

'You can be *married* any time you like. But if you're talking about a public wedding, postpone it.'

'Why?'

'Being a bridegroom is a tough assignment. You won't be strong enough.'

'What do you bet me?'

The stern face relaxed a little.

'I don't bet with patients. And I certainly wouldn't begin with such a determined man as you, Mr Egerton. You will be going home tomorrow, all being well. Your GP will be in charge of the case. You must be guided by him.'

And Dr Croft stalked out, followed by his acolytes. He was left to his perplexities. When Anthea returned, he voiced them.

'The doctor said that I would be going home tomorrow. But how can I? I don't think I could even get out of bed at present.'

'But you'll go by ambulance.'

'How? Will they come and fetch me here?'

182

'Of course not. We'll take you, in bed, down to casualty.'
He tried to visualize the process.
'You mean, there is a lift large enough to take a bed?'
She looked at him pityingly
'Haven't you ever been in a proper hospital before?'
'I've never been in a hospital at all, proper or otherwise.
At least, not since I was born . . .'

Amanda was there to give him his lunch. This time, he tried
to raise his hand to help guide the spoon to his mouth. He
only succeeded in spilling it. She mopped up with a tissue.
'That's fine. Shows you're getting a little strength back.
Let's try again. Oh, perhaps you'd like to be propped up a
bit more. I'll rearrange the pillows.'
Afterwards, exploring the new confidence that was estab-
lishing itself between them, he said tentatively, 'Would you
mind doing a tiresome little chore for me? My fingernails
are getting long.'
'Of course. I may have pliers and an emery board in my
bag. Otherwise, I can get them from the hotel room – yes,
here they are.'
He watched her pretty hands at work.
'How do you get that lovely soft sheen on your own nails?
It's not varnish, is it?'
'No. Messy stuff. I just polish them.'
'They look like luscious pink lollipops.'
'Don't try them. They're not edible.'
'I can see. They're sharp. I must think twice before I fall
out with you, my beauty.'
As she was completing the manicure, a further offering
of flowers was brought in, a large pot plant.
She looked at the label.
'From Kevin and Ruth Harris. Who are they, darling?'
'I've no idea. I don't know anybody of that name. It must
be a mistake.'
But she was already unpacking the plastic covering. And
a splendid pink azalea was revealed.
'There's a letter to you, tied to the plant.'

She opened it, and held it up so that they both could read it.

It was written, in a careful, rather clerkly hand, from a modest address in the same neighbourhood as Mrs Howard's flat, and ran:

Dear Mr Egerton,

I must thank you – though any thanks are inadequate – for your courageous and effective intervention on my behalf on Sunday night. These blackguards have a grudge against me and I was in great danger.

I learnt of your identity from the police, and have been inquiring after you each day at the hospital. I was immensely relieved to be told this morning that you had begun to recover.

This plant comes as a token from my wife and myself of our enormous gratitude and admiration, which we hope some time to be able to express to you in person.

Yours sincerely,
Kevin Harris.

Amanda flushed with pleasure.

'How *lovely*. Darling, I *am* proud of you. We must take great care of the azalea. We must take it home, whatever we do with the cut flowers. I'm sure they would let us take it in the ambulance.'

'But what on earth shall we do with it? It would be terribly in the way in my room.'

'It could be planted out.'

'There's hardly room to swing a cat in the Provost's garden.'

'I could take it home and ask Daddy to look after it. He would be thrilled. And eventually we could have it in pride of place at West Grove, couldn't we?'

'How sentimental you are, darling. But do as you like.'

'And may I write and thank them, as I have done with the other people who have sent flowers and cards?'

'Please do. I'm sure you'll think of something nice to say.'

'And I hope you won't think it sentimental if we keep the letter? May I leave it by your bedside for the moment?'

'As you wish. And they tell me that I am going to be taken home – that is, I suppose, to the Lodgings – by ambulance tomorrow.'

'That's right. I shall go with you.'

'Good. But, darling, how shall I manage when I leave hospital? I can't do *anything* for myself at the moment.'

'Your father has been on to the college doctor. A nurse will be there.'

'That sounds all right. Now, *do* go and get yourself a proper lunch. And go out. Have a walk in the park.'

She let herself be persuaded.

In the early afternoon there was a knock on his door. He was amazed to see Fred walk in.

'I say. What brings you to London?'

'You, of course.'

'You haven't come specially to see me?'

'Yes, I have. We've been in a tremendous way about you since J.E. telephoned. When we heard that you could have visitors, Mary and I agreed I must come up at once. Actually, I *have* combined it with a little errand for her: she wants a *hat*, which she bought last summer for Ascot, altered to wear at your wedding, so I've taken it to her milliner. I've brought you some strawberries from the garden.'

'That's very kind of you. And thank you for the flowers.'

'Were they all right?' Fred strolled over, inspected the lilies, and nodded. 'Not too bad. One never knows with these Interflora people.' He came back, and looked curiously at his brother.

'That's a nasty head wound. Does it hurt a lot?'

'Like Hell to start with. Not too bad now.' John reminded himself that Fred might have seen active service, and added, 'I expect you've had to look at worst things.'

'Yes, I have. But it's different when it's in the family.'

Then the door opened.

'The police to see you.'

185

John effected introductions.

'This is my brother, Captain Egerton.'

'Would you like me to go, Inspector?' asked Fred.

'You can stay if you like, Captain. I expect you've heard it all already.'

'No, I haven't. I only heard in the merest outline from my father.'

'Could you find another chair, Fred?'

The inspector had been given some facts by the Provost. He had Mrs Howard's name and address and knew that John had been attending a dinner party at her flat on the night of the incident.

'Shall we take it from there? Take your time. I know you've been very ill.'

In answer to the questions asked, he related his story.

'And what happened afterwards,' he said, in conclusion, 'you will have to tell *me*. Because I don't remember any more.'

He was asked if he could give a description of the criminals, realizing that it was dark and that they were masked. He thought they were white, not black. He thought they were about his own height. He had heard the second man say a few words, he would not offend their ears by repeating them, but could not identify the accent, except that it was common south Midlands. That apparently tallied with what Mr Harris remembered.

'And he was all right? Not hurt?'

'He was unhurt. Only very shaken. As soon as they let go of him to deal with you, he raced for his life down the mews into the main street and dialled 999 from the nearest call box. When the police got there, they found you lying in the gutter in a pool of blood and the two thugs gone. They gave you what first aid they could and of course sent urgently for an ambulance.'

'I had a charming letter from Mr Harris, with flowers, this morning. He spoke of them being people who had a grudge against him. Do you know what he meant? Have a look at the letter. It's just there, by the bed.'

The inspector picked it up, read it, and smiled.

'Very nice. He's a very nice man. Too nice to have understood what a nasty world we live in. Yes, we know all about this. It's a long story. But in brief . . .'

It was an ugly story. The two men were evidently members of a gang which had carried out a number of particularly brutal armed robberies. Most recently they had attacked the firm where Mr Harris worked. Thanks to his presence of mind, the police were able to make an arrest. Before the trial, Mr Harris began to get threatening phone calls. They knew that he was the key witness for the prosecution. They said they would "beat all Hell out of him" if he testified. He was provided with some discreet police protection. He gave his evidence in court, gave it very well. The man was convicted and sent to prison. Mr Harris thought it was all over. But the police warned him to be prudent. For a time he followed their advice. Then he got careless. He had taken to visiting his mother regularly on Sunday night. They were watching him and were on the lookout for a chance to ambush him. That night, he stayed late with his mother and, being in a hurry to get back, he without thinking took the short cut home. That was it.

'Would they have killed him?' asked John. 'They had knives . . .'

'Those people probably carry knives routinely. They were going to do what they had threatened. Gag and tie him, drag him out of the way, probably into one of those small yards at the back of the mews, and beat him up. He would have had a very bad time. Possibly have been maimed for life.'

Fred intervened.

'May I ask a question? These vindictive swine: is there any risk that they might hold it against my brother that he helped Mr Harris to escape?'

'I don't think so. Their logic would be, that he was a complete stranger who had blundered into a settling of accounts which didn't concern him. They wouldn't go to all that trouble out of spite. Seizing Mr Harris must have cost them a lot of organization.'

187

'Wasn't getting Mr Harris sheer spite, though?'

'No. Of course it was a revenge attack. But they meant to intimidate him and his like from disregarding their threats – from collaborating with the police.'

'Will they try to get him again?'

'Yes. If we don't get *them* first. But at least he'll be on his guard.'

The inspector got up to go.

'You couldn't have taken on more dangerous men. But it was a brave thing to do.'

'What else could I have done?'

'A good many people would have turned tail when they saw what was going on. Perhaps have salved their conscience by going away and telephoning the police. It would certainly have been too late to save Kevin Harris.'

After the inspector had gone, Fred asked whether he might read Mr Harris's letter . . .

'You did very well, John. What a dark horse you are.'

'If it had been you, you would have probably knocked both of them out straight away. You're the pugilist of the family.'

'Only,' said Fred, modestly, 'in the sense that "a good big 'un is better than a good smaller 'un" – was it Tom Cribb who said that?'

'You and Richard have always talked about me as if I were a pygmy,' said John, suddenly irritable.

'Have we? 'Fred was surprised. 'I suppose you were a little boy to us for so long . . . Well, time marches on . . .'

Even with the support of Amanda's presence, he found the journey extremely tiring. The noise and the vibration got on his nerves, in his low state. He only just found the strength to thank the ambulance crew who had brought him and carried him on a stretcher up to his room. He saw that there was a nurse waiting. He heard his father's voice. He was conscious of being put to bed. Then he slid into a deep sleep.

How long after that he did not know, he heard a cheerful

voice beside him say, 'Well, you *have* been in the wars. How do you feel now?'

He opened his eyes, and saw the familiar figure of the college doctor.

'Not too bad, thanks. A bit limp . . .'

He spent most of the following day asleep.

A large, business-like woman woke him next morning, saying, 'Would you like to try getting out of bed?'

She had brought a walking frame, and, having helped him to swing his legs over the side of the bed, got him to his feet, holding on to it. With her assistance he managed to take the few steps needed to cross the passage over to the bathroom. He subsided, feeling very shaky, on the bathroom stool. Swiftly and efficiently, she washed him all over, dried him, shaved him, and returned him to bed. He found the scent of his own aftershave and talcum powder an agreeable change from hospital smells.

'And if you want me for anything else, use the mobile phone,' she said, finally. 'It's by your pillow.'

After breakfast the Provost came up, bringing some letters and the newspapers.

'Shall I open the letters that have come for you?'

'Yes, please do. Like old times, J.E.'

They discussed the letters. Then his father read aloud some extracts from the papers. John was keen to catch up with the financial news.

'I suppose we haven't yet had the result of the structural survey I ordered of West Grove and of the other house in that street?'

'No. But you ought to get it pretty soon, oughtn't you? You've used these surveyors before?'

'Many times. And there's really no hurry. I can't think there is much danger of gazumping in this case. And we've got the flat in Town for a year. Amanda has seen and approved it. But West Grove would be nice, eventually.'

'It sounds charming. Now, John, don't tire yourself. I'll come again later in the morning. Dr Austin is going to call again, some time before lunch.'

189

Some time afterwards, his phone rang. It was Greenfield.

'Good morning, Mr John. I'm sorry to disturb you. Mr Miller is here asking to see you. He will quite understand if you are not having visitors yet. Shall I show him up?'

'Mr Miller?' John was surprised. But he agreed.

'Yes, please send him up. He knows the way.'

Alban appeared. He seemed flustered at seeing John and left the door open behind him.

'Nice of you to come,' murmured John. 'Sit down.'

'I hope you are better,' he said, formally. 'I came to tell you two pieces of news. One is, that I have got my Ph.D.'

'Congratulations. I hope you are going to publish the thesis?'

'Thank you, yes. I have plans for publication.'

'I shall look forward to reading it. I have always admired Berthe Morisot.'

Alban disregarded what he said, and went on. 'The other is, that I shall shortly be announcing my engagement to the daughter of one of my parents' closest friends. My father has always wished me to marry her and she is willing. I asked her yesterday.'

'Congratulations again. It sounds an admirable arrangement.'

Miller showed signs of irritation.

'You can afford to take it lightly.'

'You wouldn't wish me to take it *au tragique*?'

Miller said, inconsequently, 'Last Monday, rumours were flying round the college that you had been killed.'

'Really? No doubt a garbled version of something that Mrs Macrae had told somebody.' He smiled. 'You must have been disappointed when you heard that it wasn't true.'

Miller's face darkened.

'Can't you take *anything* seriously? You slick, flippant, cynical reptile.' Then his self-control broke down completely. 'I hate you. *God*, how I hate you!'

At that moment, John saw Amanda, horrified, in the open doorway.

'Alban!' she said.

Miller jumped like a shot rabbit. He got up from the bedside, where he had been sitting and faced her.

'I didn't come here to make a scene,' he yelped. 'That wasn't my intention. I came to tell him – what you already know – that I have got my Ph.D. And,' he made an effort to be calm, 'that I am now engaged to the girl my parents have always wished me to choose. It's not my fault if we quarrelled. John taunted me.'

Amanda said indignantly, 'Leave John in peace and go away.'

'Very well. I'll leave you to your toy boy.'

'You don't know what you're saying.'

Her voice was cold with contempt.

'You're right. I don't. I don't.'

He looked desperately from her to John, and back to her. Abruptly, he dropped on one knee in front of her, lifted the hem of her skirt to his lips and kissed it. Then he rushed out.

'Poor chap,' said John, mildly. 'But for the grace of God, and of Amanda, there go I. I knew he had taken our engagement very badly. He told me so at the time. He thought that you would have ended by accepting him if I hadn't been there. Then apparently in the confusion on Monday there was a rumour that I was dead. I suppose that raised false hopes. I shouldn't have teased him. I can only imagine what I should have felt myself if I had lost you to someone else.'

'You are magnanimous, darling. I couldn't have *believed* that he would behave so badly. When I came in, he looked as if he was going to strangle you. When you were lying defenceless in bed.'

'Perhaps he was. You must have left a trail of disconsolate admirers behind you. Let's hope the others aren't so violently disposed.'

A little pacified, she sat down beside him.

'I had made plans to go home today, for a few days. I have a fitting of my dress, and a lot of wedding presents to open and acknowledge. I told Mummy that I should have to consult you.'

191

'Of course you must go. I'm afraid I can't offer to drive you.'

'There's a coach at 2 o'clock. I shall go by that. No trouble. I shall take the azalea. Daddy would love to look after it for us. But before I leave you . . . Mummy is worried about the wedding.'

'I'm sorry. What's the matter?'

'She wonders whether we ought not to postpone it, as it's so soon after your accident. If we changed the date now, to a few weeks later, she would have time to let people know and you wouldn't have to risk letting anyone down.'

'I don't care a damn about letting people down. Why *will* you persist in thinking that I am unselfish? What I mind about is getting married to you.'

'But John, do you really think you will be well enough?'

'Of course I shall be well enough. Leave it to me.'

'Will you at least ask the doctor what he thinks? You must think of your health.'

'Of course I'll ask the doctor. Anything you like. Only not putting off the wedding.'

She looked at him for a few moments in perplexity.

'And then there is the honeymoon.'

'What about it?'

'We were going to drive to London and get *Le Shuttle* and drive across France and to Italy, as far as Florence. Naturally I could drive some of the way. But it is a really terribly strenuous programme. And doing all this sightseeing. And going round picture galleries. Then, we have to move into the flat. And start work.'

He moved fretfully.

'Couldn't we leave it until nearer the time and see how I am?'

'But we've booked the tickets and reserved rooms at a lot of hotels, with a deposit, haven't we? If we left it until the last moment, we shouldn't get our money back, should we?'

'Ah, that's a point,' John agreed. 'How practical you are, my dear. Yes, I suppose we ought to reconsider our plans while we can still cancel. But think of all the lovely things we were going to see. Wouldn't you be disappointed?'

'I know we both will be disappointed,' she said, at once. 'But we must wait until you've got your strength back. Please God, we have all the rest of our lives to do these things.'

'Well, I suppose we had better play for safety. I shall have a lot of letters to write, to do all this cancelling.'

'Your father, when I mentioned the problem to him, said he was sure Mrs Macrae would write the letters, and you would only have to sign them: she isn't very busy at the moment.'

'All right. The correspondence is all in the right-hand drawer of my desk. Take it and give it to J.E. But what shall we do instead?'

'Shall I look out for a nice hotel in the country or by the seaside, with a swimming pool, naturally, and not too far away, so that we could drive or get ourselves driven there as soon as the toasts and the cake-cutting were over and we had changed?'

'I suppose so. It doesn't sound exciting.'

'And then you could really convalesce. Rest and eat and swim . . .'

'And make love,' said John, suddenly less peevish.

They smiled at each other.

Later in the morning, the Provost brought the doctor up. He professed himself well-pleased with his patient's progress.

'But I am glad to hear,' he said, 'that you have decided on a more reposing honeymoon than careering over France and Italy. And what about the wedding itself? I know, as you have been so kind as to invite my wife and myself, that it is to be here at St Matthew's, which will make it less arduous for you. Do you really think, though, that you should stick to that date?'

'Why not?'

'Well, on medical grounds I would advise putting it off until later. Unless you're prepared to come in a wheelchair.'

'I am determined to be well. What I think would help is, if I could start swimming again as soon as possible.'

193

'It could do you nothing but good. But you would have to have someone to take you there and go in with you.'

'We might be able to recruit someone,' observed his father. 'Some needy graduate or even undergraduate, provided he is responsible and can swim, might be glad to earn a little money that way. The trouble is, there are not many people around at this stage of the vacation.'

'There is Gervase Ward,' said the doctor, thoughtfully. 'He is a medical student about to begin the final year of clinical work, who is with me for a few weeks to see if he likes general practice. I couldn't put any pressure on him. But I could ask him.'

'Please do,' said John. 'That would be splendid.'

'And we must offer him a suitable fee,' remarked the Provost. 'It will take at least an hour of his time. Perhaps we could put our heads together about that before you go, Robert.'

'Oh, and there is one other thing,' exclaimed John. 'I need a wig. I don't mind being a skinhead in the baths, but I don't want to frighten people here unnecessarily with this awful bruise and the scar, until my hair has grown again. What do I do to get one?'

'No problem. I'll see to that. You should get it quite quickly.'

That evening, the doctor rang up. He had spoken to Gervase Ward after his surgery. In principle, the young man was quite willing. He thought it would be best, though, if they met to discuss it. Could be come round about 8.30?

At 8.30 someone came up the staircase two steps at a time. There was a knock on the door and Ward breezed in.

He sat down and began to go over what would be required. They got on well. He said he would do it, in the early afternoon, for the week that he would still be with Dr Austin.

'The only snag is,' he explained, 'I've got to go into the pool with you, and I haven't got bathing things here. Could you lend me something?'

John shook his head, smiling. Ward was a big man.

194

'Nothing that would fit, I'm afraid. Why not go out and buy what you need, and put it down to your expense account with me?'

They agreed that he would call at 2 o'clock the next day.

'And I'd like to take you in my car, rather than have a taxi, if there's room to park outside the baths. It's an old rattletrap, but we shall be sure of being able to come straight back with no risk of being kept waiting.'

John managed better the next morning, and asked to dress. He found this a more athletic process than he had expected. In particular, pulling on his trousers was quite a struggle, even with help. However, he achieved it and was pleased to be sitting up in his clothes. The more so because he had a visit in the course of the morning from Mrs Macrae, who had come to check with him the letters she had written on his behalf and get them signed. Very professional as always, she did not turn a hair at the sight of him and asked kindly after his health. He was aware that, in bathing shorts, he would appear an even stranger sight, black and blue with bruises. Ward, who had no doubt seen much worse cases in hospital, was unconcerned. And there happened to be no other customers at the baths at that moment. But a member of the staff, who was on duty, was amazed.

'John Egerton? I thought I hadn't seen you for some days. What ever have you done to yourself?'

'I've had a tiff with some thugs. I've come to begin a spot of rehabilitation,' said John, airily.

'Do you want any help?'

'I don't think so, thank you. As you see, I've got a substantial minder.'

The familiar environment gave him confidence. And at first the caress of the water on his skin was as welcoming as ever. When he began to swim it was painfully different. At the first movement of the gentlest breast-stroke the deeply bruised muscles of shoulder, arm and side protested violently. He forced himself to go on. It was torture. After a few moments he was obliged to give up.

He gasped, 'I can't do any more.'

Ward brought him safely to the side.

'Wait here a few moments, while I dry myself and dress. I'll come and help you then and we can go straight back.'

Unutterably dejected, John sat dripping and shivering, with his hands over his face. He could not make his body do as he wanted. For the first time, he began to doubt his ability to recover in time for the wedding. The prospect of having to postpone it, or go to it in a wheelchair, which he had brushed aside, now loomed up as a real and sickening possibility. He admitted to himself that his self-confidence had in it an element of bravado.

Then Ward arrived and took him off to dry him and help him to dress, put him in the car and drove him back to the Lodgings. As he entered the hall, on Ward's arm, he subsided on to a chair.

'I feel tired,' he said. 'I shall rest for a few minutes. Don't let me keep you. My father will give me a hand upstairs.'

Without a word, Ward picked him up as if he had been a child, carried him up the two flights of stairs and deposited him in his armchair.

'I'm too heavy,' John protested.

'On the contrary, you're much too light,' replied Ward. 'You need to put on weight. Have a rest now.'

He propped up John's feet on a stool, and covered him with the throw from the bed.

'See you tomorrow,' he said, and departed.

John went to sleep almost before he had gone.

When he next looked at his watch, he found that he had slept for almost four hours. He was rather stiff, and ravenously hungry. When his supper arrived, he wolfed it.

Afterwards the Provost looked in.

'How did it go? I hope you didn't tire yourself?'

'Not quite so well as I had hoped,' he answered, cautiously. 'Hardly more than a paddle. But it's a start.'

'It was sporting of you to go at all. Robert Austin's boy looked after you all right?'

'Very well indeed.'

'He put his head round the door before leaving to tell

me that he had left you to rest. So I didn't disturb you. Amanda rang up after lunch.'

'I *am* sorry I missed her. What a damn nuisance.'

'She was staggered to hear that you had gone swimming. Well she might be. She will phone tomorrow before dinner. She is out to supper with neighbours this evening. She sent all her love, of course.'

He was almost able to wash and dress unaided the following day, although he was extremely slow. He told himself that it was foolish to panic. He must train. Methodically.

He tried moving his arms above his head. It hurt. But he persevered. And when Ward arrived, he consulted him about these exercises. Ward suggested some refinements. He entered into the spirit of the scheme.

'Are you going for gold?' he asked, jokingly, and took him off to the baths.

This time, he almost managed to reach the other end, though it was pain and grief, and the effort left him exhausted for the time being. He took heart.

And in the evening he had a welcome visitor in the shape of Jonathan Sopes.

He was visibly shocked by John's appearance.

'You really *have* been in a fight,' he commented, 'And a fight with knives, too. I shall have to tell my people, England's no safer than Jamaica. But John, will you be all right for the wedding?'

'*Et tu, Brute?* Yes. Don't worry. I may look an awful sight still, but I am really very much better.'

Jonathan seemed reassured.

'You did me the honour of asking me to be your best man,' he said. 'Now, I think in both our countries it is the custom for the bridesmaids to receive a present from the best man. And Amanda tells me she is having two: your little nieces Louise and Anne. So I asked her advice on the choice of a present.'

'How good of you to think of it.'

'And in the end she came with me to choose it.'

Amanda and Jonathan going shopping together? . . .

197

'This is ridiculous,' he said to himself. 'I'm getting jealous already. Emily was quite right.'

But he said aloud, 'What a splendid idea. May I ask what you chose?'

'I'll show you.' Jonathan produced two little jewellers' boxes and carefully took the contents out.

A small bar brooch glinted on the table, decorated with a gothic capital L. The other was identical, but with the letter A.

'Amanda said it needn't be anything expensive. That it was just a token.'

John admired them.

'I'm sure the girls will be delighted. I expect they will be among the first, if not the very first, pieces of jewellery of their own they have ever had. And they couldn't have anything prettier.'

'And I asked Amanda whether I should have them sent to your brother and sister-in-law. But she thought it would be nicer for me to give them to the girls in person, just before the wedding.'

'I hope you will. Mary can be told to expect them. And I'm sure Amanda will organize an opportunity to meet them.'

'Good. And I think my only duty apart from that is to come into chapel with you and hand the ring to you at the right moment? Will there be one ring or two?'

'I must ask Amanda. The older generation in England tended to regard the bride's ring as the symbol of the marriage. But in a lot of European countries married men wear a ring and the custom is spreading here.'

'The Provost wears a ring, though?'

'He wears a signet ring. So does Amanda's father. But you must stand by me, Jonathan, in every sense of the word. Please come to my room at the least half an hour before.'

'Count on me, John. Anything I can do. Now or at any time.'

*   *   *

198

By the next morning, Mrs Mace was impatient to clean the room. Initially, his injuries having appealed to her sense of the dramatic, she had been indulgent – almost motherly. Seeing that he had been able to dress and 'go gallivantin' off to the baths,' she reverted to her normal imperiousness.

The Provost suggested coming down and sitting out in his small walled garden. He helped him to bring down his mail, his newspapers, and his mobile telephone, and provided a deckchair and cushions.

There was a good news about West Grove. Mrs Millett's solicitor wrote that she was willing to sell him the cottage as well as the house for the sum he had offered, on condition that Miss Perkins was guaranteed the right to live there at a reasonable rent. A search had established that the house itself was not a listed building, still less so the more ordinary house in the same street which he had decided to buy. It meant that planning permission was going through without a hitch. The result of the structural survey showed that West Grove, though in bad condition, was basically a well-built house and free from anything like dry rot. He rang up his builders and confirmed that the job could begin as soon as they were free, by which time he expected to be able to go over the work with them.

He had a light lunch with his father downstairs. He felt more confident about appearing in public because the promised wig had arrived. The general effect was something more than tolerable, and, by combing it in a somewhat raffish style to one side, he disguised the scar on his forehead to his satisfaction. The Provost approved.

Amanda, when she returned, was quite overcome.

'Oh, don't get up, please, darling. But how wonderful you look. I couldn't have believed that a few days would make such a difference. And – that *can't* be your own hair, so soon? No, of course. But it's really *very* good. Not like your lovely silky black hair, but from a distance very convincing.'

'I'm glad you're pleased,' he said, as they sat down together. 'Tell me about yourself. How's the dress going?'

'The dress is going very well. Mummy's dress too. And Mary and I have had several talks on the phone, about the dresses for Louise and Anne.'

'And how are you and they going to meet up, on the day?'

'Very simple. I have booked rooms at the Southgate for myself and for my parents, who are staying the previous night in order to be near St Matthew's. Fred and Mary are driving over, it will mean quite an early start for them, and they will bring the bridesmaids to the hotel, at a time we haven't yet finalized.'

'What about your flat?'

'Emily and I are packing up. We have to vacate it soon. Daddy is coming over with the car to help me take my things home. Oh, and John: he and I have been to look at hotels.'

'How good of you.'

'We trawled through a lot of advertisements, and narrowed it down to a shortlist of four. Then we did some telephoning. One was already fully booked up. So we visited the other three. One of them seemed almost ideal. And I was offered a very nice room, for which they had had a cancellation. So I booked us in. I hope I have done right. I've brought some photos which we took, and the hotel brochure.'

'How well you have done for us, my darling.'

He turned over the pages and looked at the photographs.

Meanwhile, she wanted to talk about final arrangements for the wedding: the reception – the cake – flowers – photographs . . .

He listened with half an ear, enjoying the pleasure of looking at her.

'And Mary has been *so* helpful. What a dear she is. And the little girls are *sweet*. And she mentioned, darling, that you had first met them at the party she and Fred gave on Boxing Day for the family.'

'What did she tell you about the party?'

'She said what fun it had been to have you there. They, and Richard and Sue, and your father, take it in turns to provide a family party at Christmas time. They hadn't invited you to join the rota because you were a bachelor.'

He admired Mary's tact.

'And then,' continued Amanda, 'I understood what you meant about the dining room at our flat. That if we alerted the caterers soon, we could have a lunch or dinner party for twelve at Christmas. I didn't breathe a word to Mary, naturally, but you must have been thinking of this. It would be lovely to have them all at our new home, wouldn't it? They would each be four, that makes eight, and your father, nine. If you think we ought to have another lady to balance him, perhaps we could ask Mary's sister Charlotte, I met her at the christening and she is so nice, and I believe she works in London. Or Francesca Melzi.'

John had time, while she was talking, to recover his composure.

'Charlotte is in any case high on my list of guests to be invited. And what about your parents, darling? After all, they are bound to miss you, aren't they? We must bring them in.'

'How sweet of you to think of it. That would be lovely. Will you alert the caterers, then?'

John smiled. The joke was decidedly on him.

'No immediate hurry, my dear. We'll think it out. And consult J.E.'

The evening before the wedding, the Provost had the main participants to dinner.

As his guests left, he turned to John.

'Not tired? You would probably like to retire early. You've got a strenuous day in front of you.'

'I'm not tired. Just excited. And I would like to talk, J.E.'

'Let's go into the study, then.'

They both sat down.

'It will soon be a year since I came to you in the worst fix of my life. Now, according to the terms which you made for helping me out of it, I should have been free to walk out of your house at the end of a year, whether I had repaid you or not, provided I complied with your conditions.'

'That is quite correct.'

'But wasn't that taking a tremendous risk?'

'Certainly. Why should you be the only member of the family who is allowed to speculate? If the plan had failed, I should have been the poorer by the amount I had spent on your behalf. You would have been the loser too: there would have been less to divide up eventually between the three of you.'

'You hadn't cut me out of your will?'

'Don't be ridiculous. You were still one of us, though you didn't want to be.'

'But I must have seemed miles away.'

'I often thought of you. Thought of my clever, good-looking, self-willed, amusing and utterly maddening young-est son. I often wondered what you were like now. Wondered what you were doing at that moment. Wondered whether I should ever see you again. And then, characteristically, you arrived in a whirl of melodrama. I didn't know whether to laugh or cry. I only knew that I must find some way of helping you that didn't leave your victims worse off and that made you, at least for the immediate future, harmless to myself and other people.'

'And you showed nothing. J.E., you are a fraud. You always look so imperturbable. How was a mere mortal like myself, and one bad at guessing what other people are feeling, to know what was going on in your mind? Aren't *you* acting a part most of the time?'

'Self-control and acting are perhaps a bit alike. But if one can't control oneself, how can one control a situation?'

'Well, now we have got to know one another, and it was a painful process to start with, perhaps for us both, tell me what you meant when you said you had mixed motives for being willing to help me. I thought then that you were mainly getting your own back on me. I know that I was wrong. You're not vindictive. I realize that you still had some affection for me left. And I supposed at the time that you might want to avoid disagreeable publicity for the family and, indirectly, for the college. But I still don't understand why you were prepared to risk this very large sum of money.'

'There was another reason, John. I had come to feel that it may have been partly my fault that we had drifted apart.'

'*Your* fault? What could have made you think that?'

The Provost was silent for a moment.

'Since I have been here,' he said, slowly, 'I have had to listen to many stories of revolt against home and parents, or one of the parents, from students. A much larger range of experiences than one could have from one's own family and friends. And first-hand, unlike what one gets from the media or from books. In some cases there were legitimate grievances. They had been neglected, or actually ill-treated. Some had suffered from a total lack of love. That was my own experience: my father hardly ever spoke to me except to reprimand me. I put up with it as best I could. But sometimes the parents, or one of them, had been *over*-anxious to protect them, to guide them, to make companions of them. *I* was, probably, with Fred and Richard, though mercifully it worked all right with them. But this policy had grated on some high-spirited children, who wanted from an early age to be independent, to be left to find and explore their own interests. I naively supposed that what had worked with your brothers would work with you. And then, when I might, with your mother, have tried to think of something different, I was caught up in an exceptionally busy phase at my work, and you had begun spending all your vacations with Henri. And after your mother died you never came home at all.'

'I honestly don't believe that anything you could have done in the past would have made any difference. I had to get this out of my system. I could probably never have discovered the real J.E. until I was a good deal older. Until we could meet, as it were, on equal terms.'

'That may be true. And, if it had been earlier, you would probably not have met Amanda.'

'Amanda is a bonus. The supreme bonus.'

'*Felix culpa.* Which is theologians' jargon for a misdeed which eventually has happy consequences.'

'And talking of Amanda . . .'

'What else should we be talking about, the night before your wedding?'

'Well, she wants us, her and me, to give the Christmas party for the relations this year, in our new flat.'

'Have you agreed?'

'I have. What else could I do? You're invited, naturally.'

'Thank you, I accept with pleasure. That is, if we haven't quarrelled again by that time.'

'Amanda wouldn't let me. She adores you. And of course Fred and Richard eat out of her hand. She sometimes talks as if she is marrying my family, not me.'

'Don't worry. I'm sure in the next few days you will be able to demonstrate, to her entire satisfaction, that it is you she has married.'

John passed his hand thoughtfully over his chin.

'Yes. This time tomorrow, I shall be shaving for the second time, in her honour.'

'I should hope so. By the way, you haven't had any of your headaches today?'

'I had a slight one this morning. It went off quite quickly. They've almost stopped.'

'Good. Now, come along. It's time we went to bed.'

They went upstairs.

They paused on the first floor landing, as they had done for some months.

'Goodnight, John,' said the Provost.

In a rare gesture of tenderness, he put his hand for a moment on his son's shoulder.

'Goodnight. Goodbye. Good luck.'